#1 Teacher Recommended!

BRIDGING GRADES
PreK to K

Carson Dellosa Education
Greensboro, North Carolina

Caution: Exercise activities may require adult supervision. Before beginning any exercise activity, consult a physician. Written parental permission is suggested for those using this book in group situations. Children should always warm up prior to beginning any exercise activity and should stop immediately if they feel any discomfort during exercise.

Caution: Before beginning any food activity, ask parents' permission and inquire about the child's food allergies and religious or other food restrictions.

Caution: Nature activities may require adult supervision. Before beginning any nature activity, ask parents' permission and inquire about the child's plant and animal allergies. Remind the child not to touch plants or animals during the activity without adult supervision.

Caution: Before completing any balloon activity, ask parents' permission and inquire about possible latex allergies. Also, remember that uninflated or popped balloons may present a choking hazard.

The authors and publisher are not responsible or liable for any injury that may result from performing the exercises or activities in this book.

Summer Bridge®
An imprint of Carson Dellosa Education
PO Box 35665
Greensboro, NC 27425 USA

© 2015 Carson Dellosa Education. Except as permitted under the United States Copyright Act, no part of this publication may be reproduced, stored, or distributed in any form or by any means (mechanically, electronically, recording, etc.) without the prior written consent of Carson Dellosa Education.

Printed in Ningbo, Zhejiang, China • All rights reserved.   ISBN 978-1-4838-1579-4

01-0202512936

Table of Contents

Making the Most of *Summer Bridge Activities*® iv
Skills Matrix vi
Summer Reading for Everyone viii
Summer Learning Is Everywhere! x

Section I: Monthly Goals and Word List 1
Introduction to Flexibility 2
Activity Pages 3
Science Experiment 43
Fitness Activities 44
Character Development Activities 45
Outdoor Extension Activities 46

Section II: Monthly Goals and Word List 47
Introduction to Strength 48
Activity Pages 49
Science Experiment 89
Fitness Activities 90
Character Development Activities 91
Outdoor Extension Activities 92

Section III: Monthly Goals and Word List 93
Introduction to Endurance 94
Activity Pages 95
Science Experiment 135
Fitness Activities 136
Character Development Activities 137
Outdoor Extension Activities 138
Reading and Writing Activities 139
Bonus Phonics Activities 140
Bonus Handwriting Practice 144

Flash Cards
Certificate of Completion

Making the Most of *Summer Bridge Activities*®

This book will help your child review prekindergarten skills and preview kindergarten skills. Inside, find lots of resources that encourage your child to practice, learn, and grow while getting a head start on the new school year.

Just 15 Minutes a Day
...is all it takes to stay sharp with learning activities for each weekday, all summer long!

Month-by-Month Organization

Three color-coded sections match the three months of summer vacation. Each month begins with a goal-setting and vocabulary-building activity. You'll also find an introduction to the section's fitness and character-building focus.

Daily Activities

Two pages of activities are provided for each weekday. They'll take about 15 minutes to complete.

Skills for School Readiness

Help your child prepare for kindergarten by developing these skills:

- Letter recognition
- Handwriting
- Vocabulary
- Numbers and counting
- Shapes and measurement
- Fine-motor skills
- Basic concepts

© Carson Dellosa Education

Plenty of Bonus Features
...match your child's needs and interests!

Bonus Activities
Science experiments invite your child to interact with the world and build critical thinking skills. Fitness and character development activities help your child stay healthy and fit and grow in kindness, honesty, tolerance, and more.

Take It Outside!
A collection of fun ideas for outdoor observation, exploration, learning, and play is provided for each summer month.

Skill-Building Flash Cards
Cut out the cards at the back of the book. Store in a zip-top bag or punch a hole in each one and thread on a ring. Take the cards along with you for practice on the go.

Give a High-Five
...to your child for a job well done!

Star Stickers
Use the star stickers at the back of the book. Place a sticker in the space provided at the end of each day's learning activities when the pages are complete.

Praise and Rewards
After completing learning activities for a whole week or month, offer a reward. It could be a special treat, an outing, or time spent together. Praise the progress your child has made.

Certificate of Congratulations
At the end of the summer, complete and present the certificate at the back of the book. Congratulate your child for being well prepared for the next school year.

© Carson Dellosa Education

Skills Matrix

Day	Alphabet	Character Development	Classification	Colors	Fine Motor Skills	Fitness	Grammar & Language Arts	Handwriting	Measurement	Numbers & Counting	Phonics	Science	Sequencing	Shape Recognition	Visual Discrimination
1									★						★
2					★									★	
3					★									★	
4					★									★	
5					★									★	
6					★									★	
7					★					★					
8										★				★	
9				★						★				★	
10										★				★	
11										★					
12										★					★
13										★					★
14										★					
15										★					
16										★					
17				★	★					★				★	
18										★					★
19					★										★
20					★										★
BONUS	★	★			★	★				★		★		★	
1										★					
2				★						★					
3				★				★			★				
4				★				★			★				
5				★				★			★				
6				★				★			★				
7				★				★			★				
8				★				★			★				
9				★				★			★				
10								★		★	★				
11								★		★	★				

Skills Matrix

Day	Alphabet	Character Development	Classification	Colors	Fine Motor Skills	Fitness	Grammar & Language Arts	Handwriting	Measurement	Numbers & Counting	Phonics	Science	Sequencing	Shape Recognition	Visual Discrimination
12				★				★			★				
13								★			★				
14								★		★	★				
15								★	★		★				★
16							★	★			★				
17				★				★			★			★	
18			★					★			★				
19								★			★				★
20								★			★				★
BONUS	★	★	★		★	★					★	★			
1			★					★			★				
2								★			★				★
3								★			★				
4							★	★			★				
5								★		★	★				
6								★		★	★				
7								★		★	★				
8								★		★	★				
9	★						★	★							
10										★					
11			★												
12								★	★				★		
13							★		★					★	★
14											★				
15											★				
16											★				
17											★				
18											★				
19											★				
20									★		★				
BONUS		★	★		★	★	★	★		★		★			

Summer Reading for Everyone

Reading is the single most important skill for school success. Experts recommend that adults read to prekindergarten and kindergarten students for at least 10 minutes each day. Help your child choose several books from this list based on his or her interests. Choose at least one fiction (F) and one nonfiction (NF) title. Then, head to the local library to begin your reading adventure!

If you like stories about fantastic creatures...
Dragons Love Tacos by Adam Rubin and Daniel Salmieri (F)
There's a Dragon in Your Book by Tom Fletcher (F)

If you like animals...
The Mitten by Jan Brett (F)
Among a Thousand Fireflies by Helen Frost and Rick Lieder (NF)

If you like stories about adventure...
Thump, Quack, Moo: A Whacky Adventure by Doreen Cronin (F)
Roaring Rockets by Tony Mitton (NF)

If you like stories about friendship...
You Are Friendly by Todd Snow (NF)
The Things I Love About Friends by Trace Moroney (F)

If you like science...
This Little Scientist
  by Joan Holub (NF)
UP! UP! UP! Skyscraper
  by Anastasia Suen (F)

If you like stories about imagination...
Harold and the Purple Crayon
  by Crockett Johnson (F)
The Rainbow Fish
  by Marcus Pfister (NF)

If you like rhymes...
Chicka Chicka Boom Boom
  by Bill Martin Jr. and
  John Archambault (F)
My Shadow
  by Robert Louis Stevenson (NF)

If you like sports...
Dino-Basketball
  by Lisa Wheeler (F)
Little Soccer
  by Brad Herzog (NF)

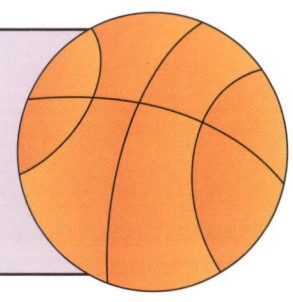

If you like funny stories...
Kitten's First Full Moon
  by Kevin Henkes (F)
Leaf Man
  by Lois Ehlert (NF)

If you like crafts and maker activities...
I'm Not Just a Scribble
  by Diane Alber (F)
The Cardboard Box Book
  by Roger Priddy and Sarah Powell (NF)

© Carson Dellosa Education

Summer Learning Is Everywhere!

Find learning opportunities wherever you go, all summer long!

Reading

- Point out words on signs, pamphlets, and posters in your child's favorite places.
- Read a nonfiction text such as a weather report together and talk about it.

Language Arts

- Trade letters, emails, or texts with a friend or relative to share summer adventures. Include stories, poems, facts, drawings, and photos.
- Work with your child to write a newsletter for family members or neighbors.

Math

- Play math games in the car. Have each person choose an object, such as blue cars, to count; the winner has a higher number at the end of the trip.
- Make a math obstacle course. Jump on sidewalk-chalked numbers, divide rocks into piles, do a number of jumping jacks to solve a problem, or meet other challenges.

Science & Social Studies

- Set up a museum on a porch or in a garage. Include leaves, flowers, insects, feathers, rocks, and more. Write a sign giving facts about each thing. Invite visitors.
- Learn about stars, the Milky Way, meteors, the moon, and other things in space. Set up blankets under the night sky and invite friends. Teach what you learned.

Character & Fitness

- Go to a concert, festival, or parade in a neighborhood that is different from yours. Tell your family members five things you enjoyed about the experience.
- Learn how to use a new physical skill. It could be skipping rope, throwing a baseball, or even doing a new dance. Keep trying until you feel confident.

© Carson Dellosa Education

SECTION 1

Monthly Goals

A goal is something that you want to accomplish. Sometimes, reaching a goal can be hard work!

Think of three goals that you would like to set for yourself this month. For example, you may want to exercise for 10 minutes each day. Have an adult help you write your goals on the lines.

Place a sticker next to each of your goals that you complete. Feel proud that you have met your goals!

1. _____ PLACE STICKER HERE

2. _____ PLACE STICKER HERE

3. _____ PLACE STICKER HERE

Word List

The following words are used in this section. They are good words for you to know. Read each word aloud with an adult. When you see a word from this list on a page, circle it with your favorite color of crayon.

big	little
circle	same
color	shape
count	trace
draw	write

© Carson Dellosa Education

SECTION I

Introduction to Flexibility

At the end of this section are fitness and character development activities that focus on flexibility. These activities are designed to get your child moving and thinking about building her physical fitness and her character. If your child has limited mobility, feel free to modify any suggested exercises to fit their individual abilities.

Physical Flexibility

Flexibility is usually understood to mean the ability to accomplish everyday tasks easily, like bending to tie a shoe. These everyday tasks can be difficult for people whose muscles and joints have not been used and stretched regularly.

Proper stretching allows muscles and joints to move through their full range of motion, which is key to maintaining good flexibility. There are many ways that your child stretches every day without realizing it. She may reach for a dropped pencil or a box of cereal. Point out these examples to your child and explain why flexibility is important to her health and growth. Challenge her to improve her flexibility consciously. Encourage her to set a stretching goal for the summer, such as practicing daily until she can touch her toes.

Flexibility of Character

While it is important to have a flexible body, it is also important to be mentally flexible. Share with your child that being mentally flexible means being open-minded to change. Talk about how disappointing it can be when things do not go her way and that this is a normal reaction. Give a recent example of when unforeseen circumstances ruined her plans, such as having a trip to the park canceled because of rain. Explain that there will be situations in life where unexpected things happen. Often, it is how a person reacts to those circumstances that affects the desirability of the outcome. By using examples your child can relate to, you can arm her with the tools to be flexible, such as having realistic expectations, brainstorming solutions to improve a disappointing situation, and looking for good things that may have resulted from the initial disappointment.

Inner flexibility can take many forms. For example, respecting the differences of other children, sharing, and taking turns are ways that a child can practice flexibility. Encourage your child to be flexible and praise her when you see her exhibiting this important character trait.

Measurement

DAY 1

Track your growth this summer. Have an adult help you measure your height. Fill in the blank. Then, draw yourself below and color the picture.

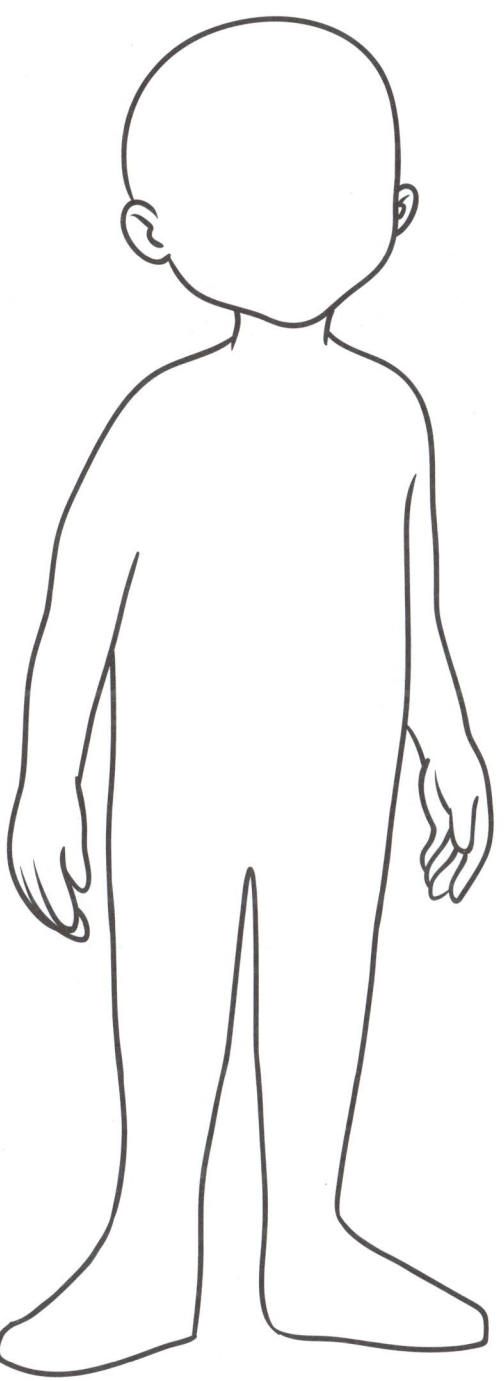

Your Height:

_____

DAY 1

Visual Discrimination

Circle the picture in each row that is the same as the first.

Fine Motor Skills

DAY 2

Trace the dashed lines.

DAY 2

Shape Recognition

This is a square.

Color the squares.

Fine Motor Skills

DAY 3

Trace the dashed lines.

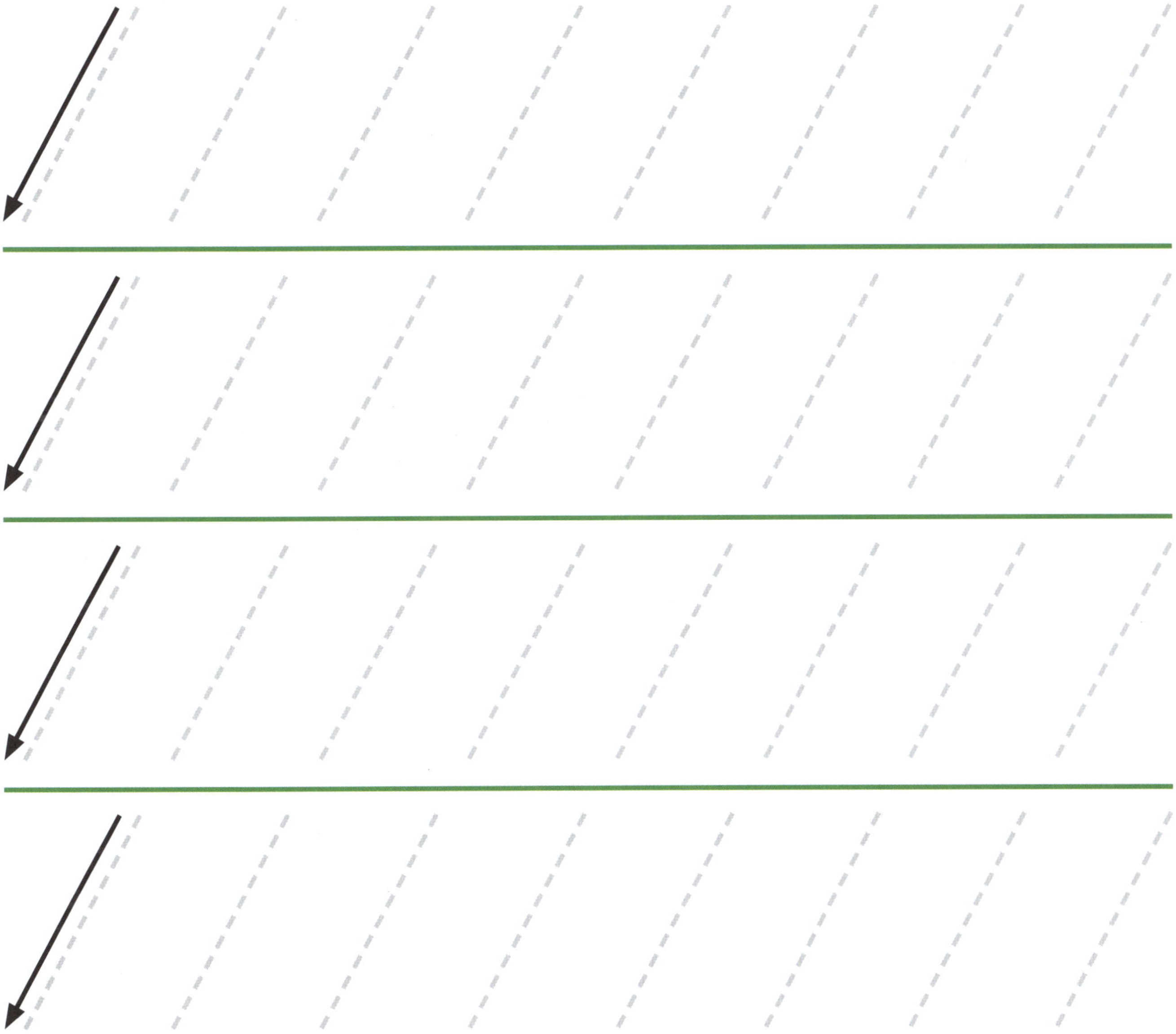

DAY 3

Shape Recognition

This is a triangle.

Color the triangles.

Fine Motor Skills

DAY 4

Trace the dashed lines.

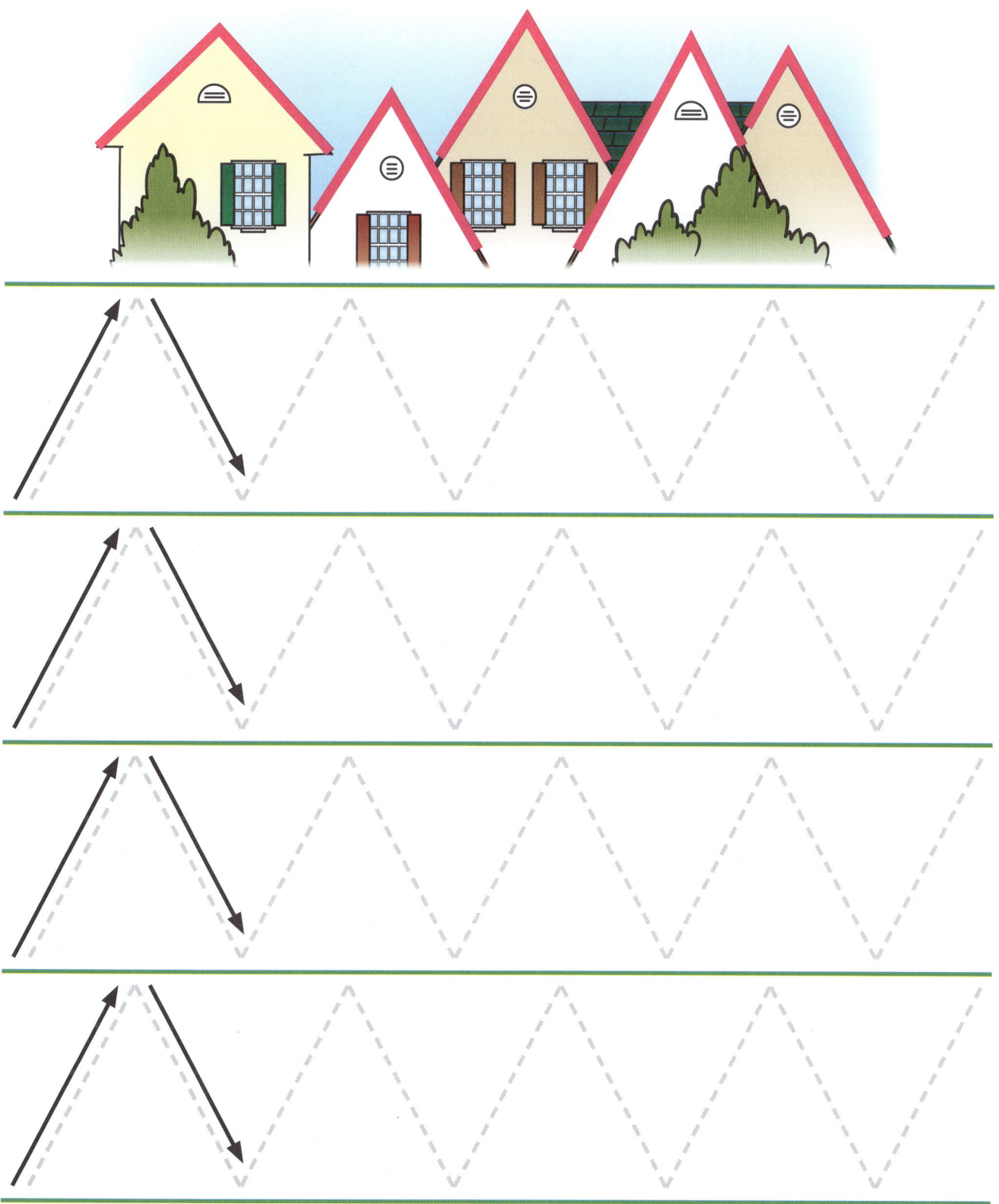

DAY 4

Shape Recognition

This is a circle.

Color the circles.

Fine Motor Skills

DAY 5

Trace the dashed lines.

DAY 5

Shape Recognition

This is a rectangle.

Color the rectangles.

Fine Motor Skills

DAY 6

Trace the dashed lines.

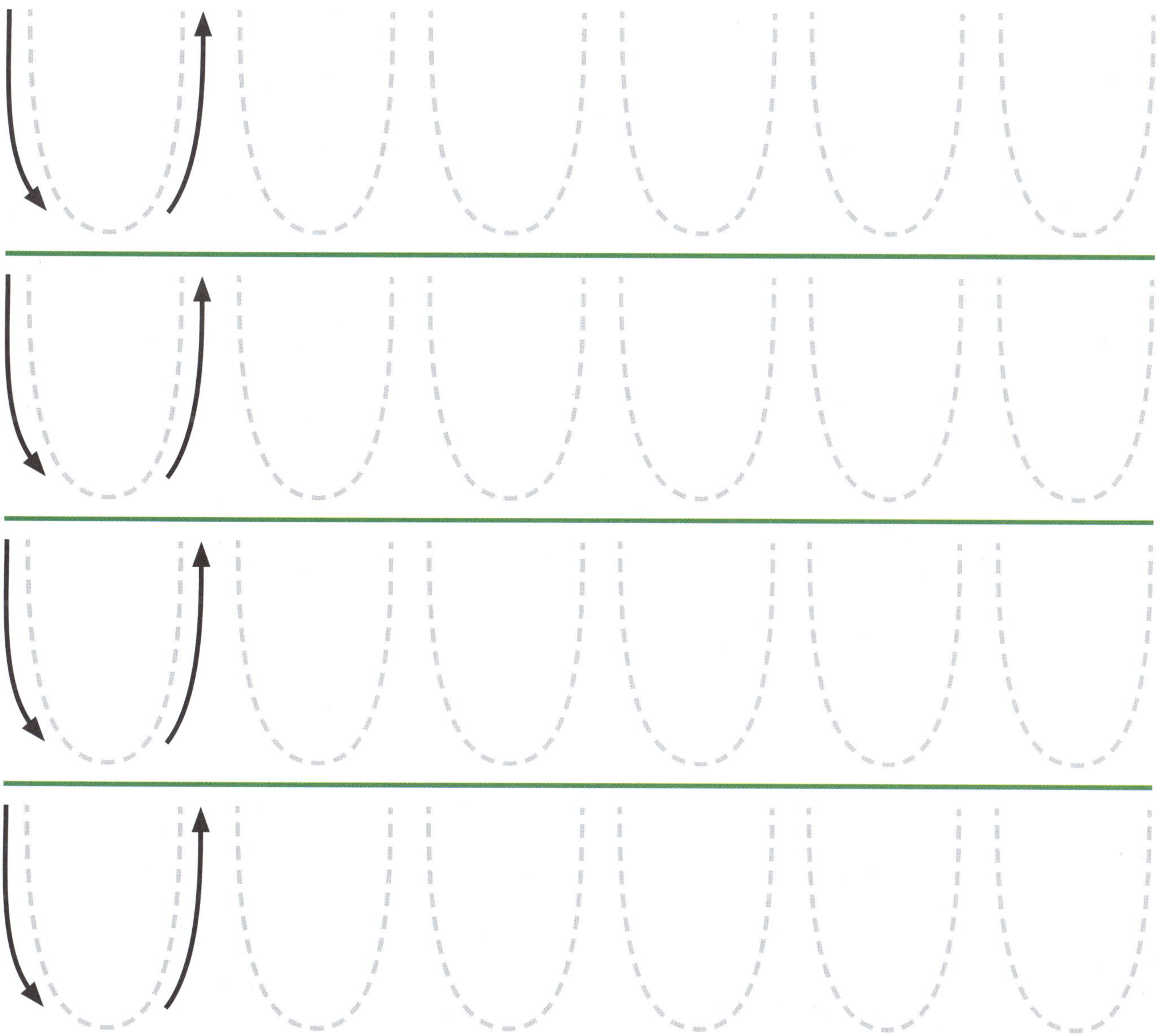

DAY 6

Shape Recognition

This is an oval.

Color the ovals.

Numbers & Counting

DAY 7

Count 1 castle.

Color 1 crown.

DAY 7

Fine Motor Skills

Use a different color of crayon to trace each kite string. Circle the child who is flying the green kite.

Numbers & Counting

DAY 8

Count 2 garages.

Color 2 cars.

DAY 8

Shape Recognition

This is a rhombus.

Color the rhombuses.

Count 3 pencils.

Color 3 books.

DAY 9

Shape Recognition/Colors

Use the key to color each shape.

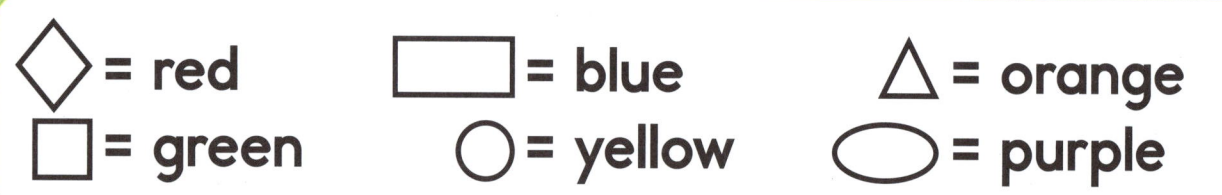

◇ = red   ▭ = blue   △ = orange
□ = green   ○ = yellow   ⬭ = purple

20
© Carson Dellosa Education

Numbers & Counting

DAY 10

Count 4 guitars.

Color 4 bells.

DAY 10

Shape Recognition

Draw an X on each object that is shaped like a circle.

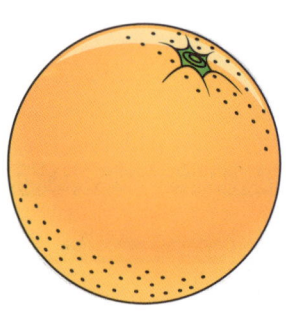

Numbers & Counting

DAY 11

Count 5 flowerpots.

Color 5 flowers.

DAY 11

Numbers & Counting

Count the objects in each row. Circle the number that tells how many objects are shown.

5 balls	1 2 3 4 5
3 suns	1 2 3 4 5
1 hat	1 2 3 4 5
2 umbrellas	1 2 3 4 5
4 pencils	1 2 3 4 5

© Carson Dellosa Education

Numbers & Counting

DAY 12

Count 6 fishbowls.

Color 6 fish.

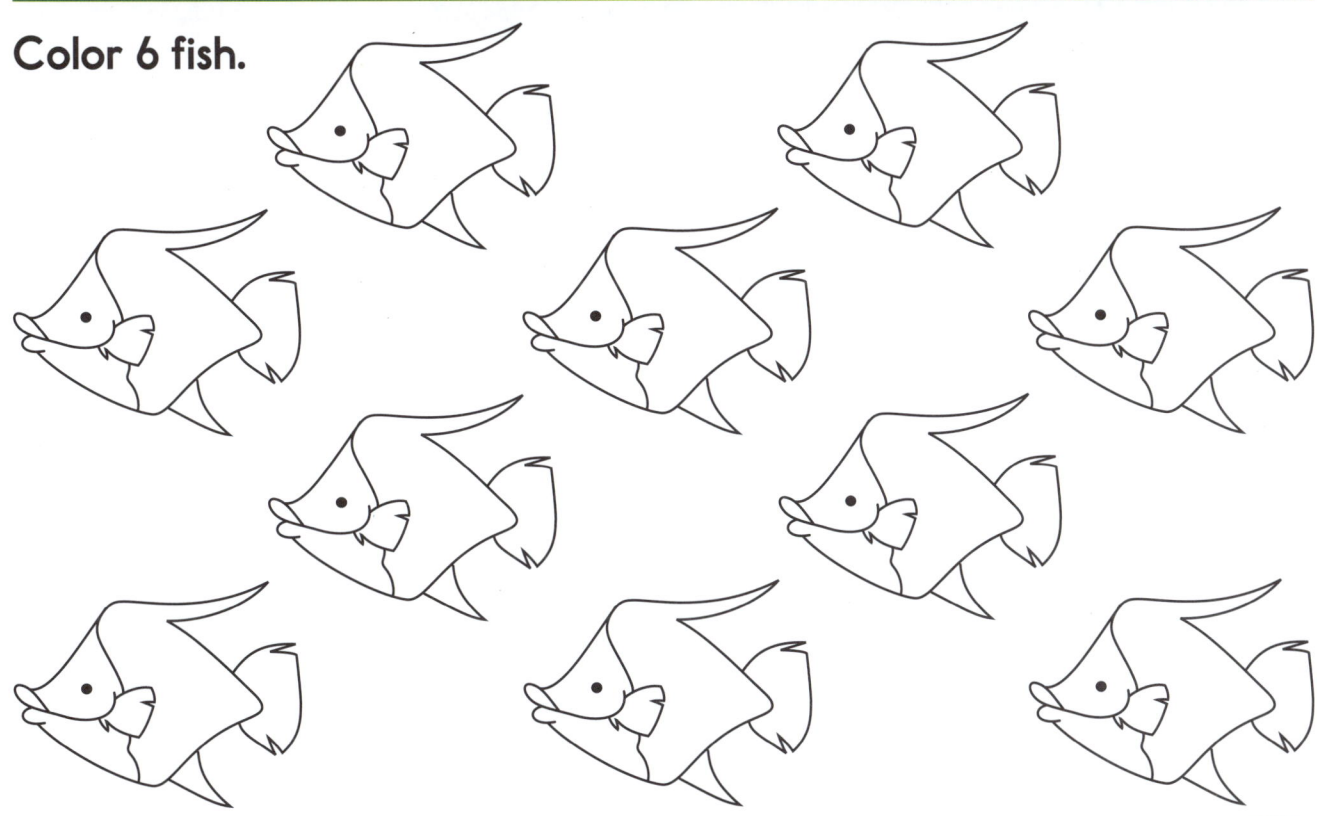

DAY 12

Visual Discrimination

Circle the objects in each set that are the same size.

Example:

Numbers & Counting

DAY 13

Count 7 umbrellas.

Color 7 clouds.

DAY 13

Visual Discrimination

Draw a line to match each big shape to the same little shape. Color the matching shapes the same color.

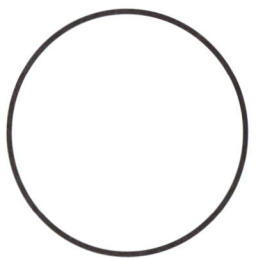 

 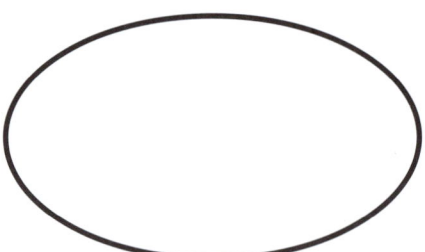

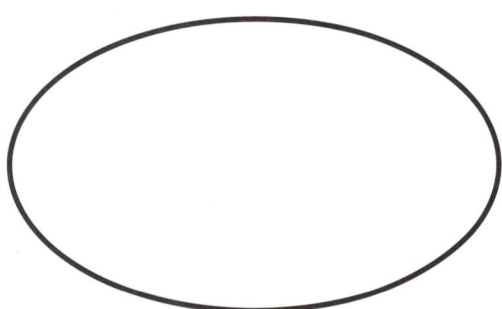 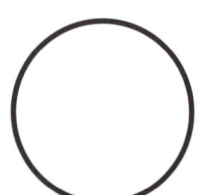

Numbers & Counting

DAY 14

Count 8 leaves.

Color 8 apples.

DAY 14

Numbers & Counting

Count the objects in each set. Write the number on the line.

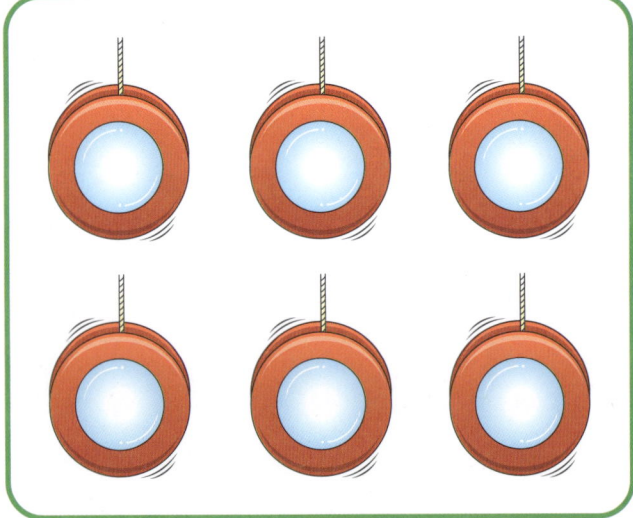

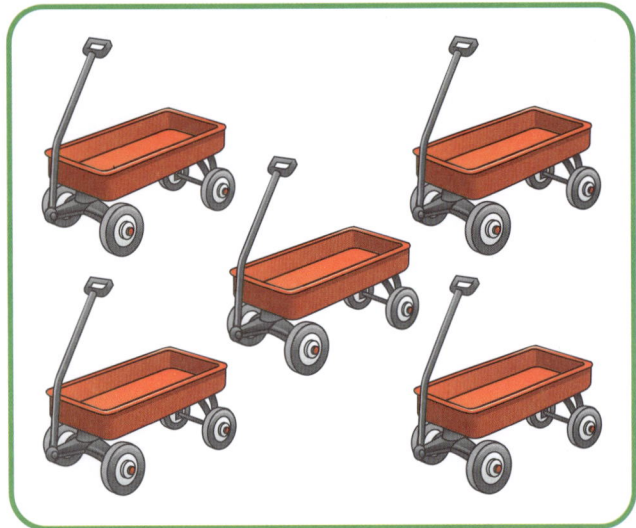

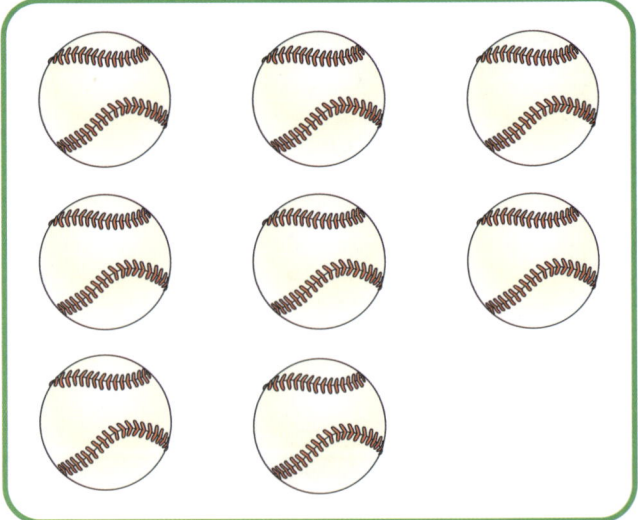

Numbers & Counting

DAY 15

Count 9 sandwiches.

Color 9 glasses of juice.

DAY 15

Numbers & Counting

Start at the ★. Connect the dots from 0 to 5. Finish coloring the picture.

Numbers & Counting

DAY 16

Count 10 paint cans.

Color 10 paintbrushes.

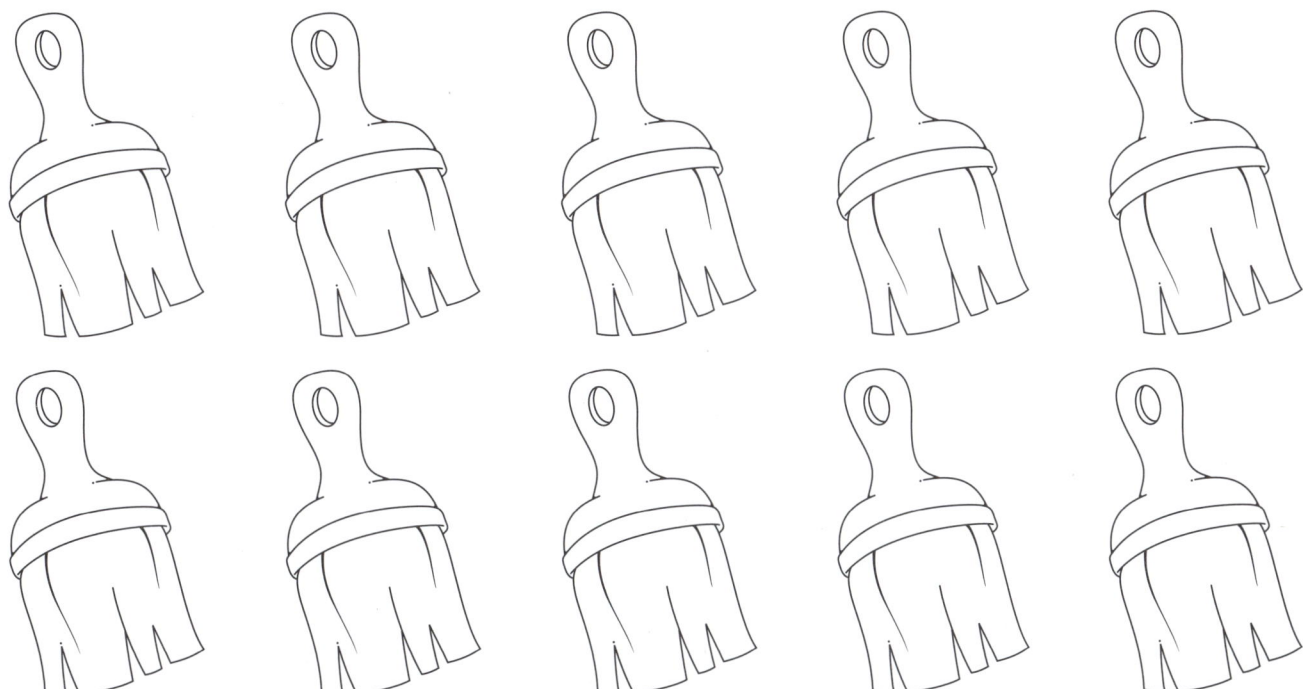

DAY 16

Numbers & Counting

Start at the ★. Connect the dots from 0 to 10. Finish coloring the picture.

Numbers & Counting/Fine Motor Skills

DAY 17

Draw a line through the numbers 0 to 10 to help the horse find the hay.

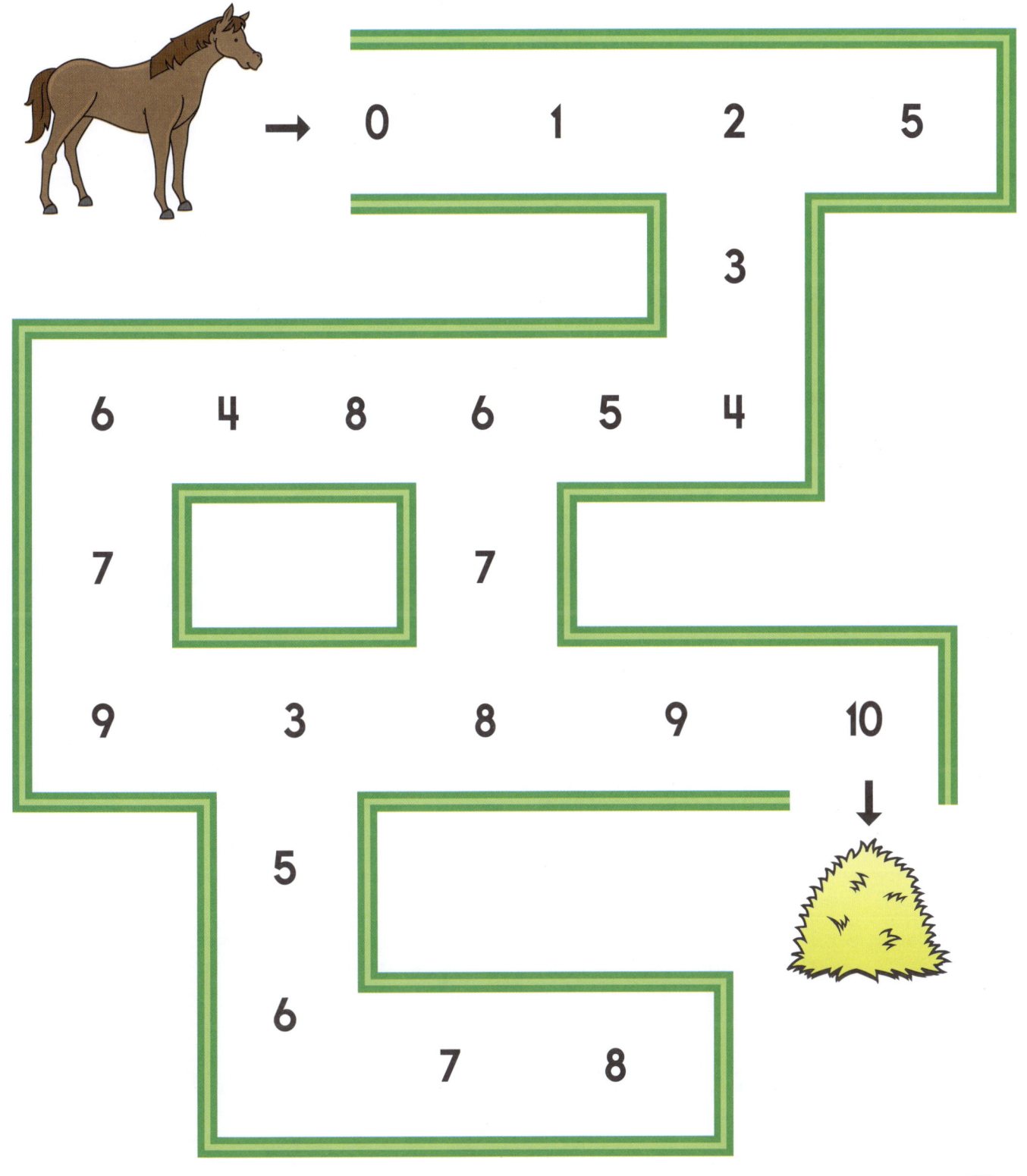

DAY 17

Shape Recognition/Colors

Use the key to color each shape.

◇ = red   □ = blue   △ = orange
□ = green   ○ = yellow   ○ = purple

Visual Discrimination

DAY 18

Draw a line in each set to match a big object to a big object. Draw a line in each set to match a little object to a little object.

Example:

DAY 18

Numbers & Counting

Count the objects in each set. Circle the number that tells how many objects are shown.

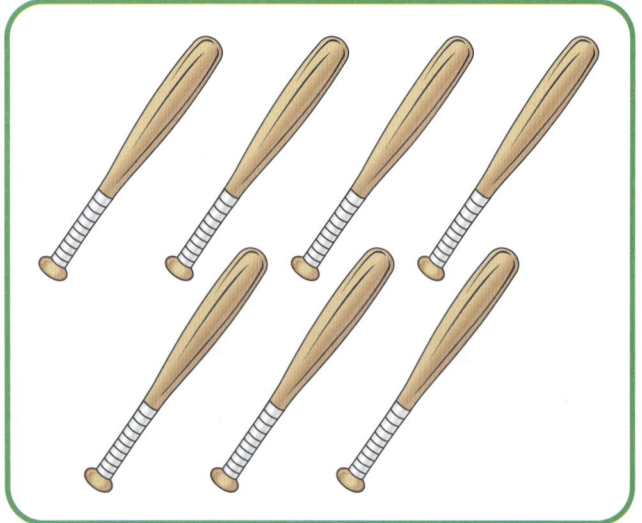

7   9   10

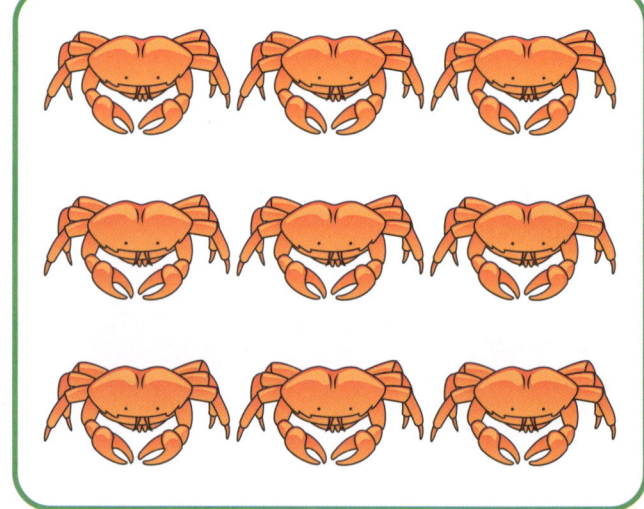

8   9   10

7   8   9

8   9   10

Visual Discrimination/Fine Motor Skills

DAY 19

Draw a line to help the dog find the bone.

DAY 19

Visual Discrimination

Color the first shape in each row. Color the matching shapes the same color.

Fine Motor Skills

DAY 20

Trace each shape with a different color of crayon.

DAY 20

Visual Discrimination

Draw a line to match each shape to an object with almost the same shape.

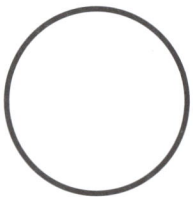

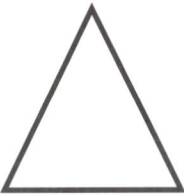

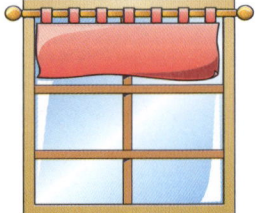

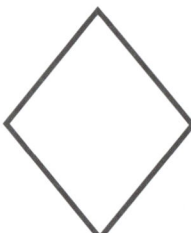

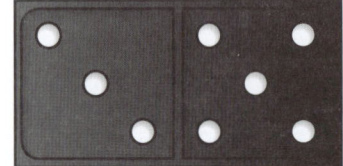

Science Experiment

Freezing Water

What happens to water when it is placed in a freezer? What happens when it is taken out of a freezer?

Materials:
- eyedropper
- ice cube tray
- water

Procedure:
Help your child use the eyedropper to place 3–5 drops of water into each section of the ice cube tray. Put the ice cube tray in the freezer for approximately 10 minutes or until the water is frozen. When frozen, remove a piece of ice from the ice cube tray and place it in your child's hand. Ask your child the questions below.

1. What happened to the water in the freezer? _____
   _____

2. What happened to the ice when you held it? _____
   _____

3. Did it take longer to freeze the water or to melt the ice? _____
   _____

4. Why do you think the water froze? _____
   _____

5. Why do you think the ice melted? _____
   _____

Fitness Activities

Stretch and Guess

Ask your child to think of three animals. How does she think these animals stretch when they wake up?

Have her practice stretching like the animals she chose. For example, if she chose a cat, she might sit on her knees and place her palms flat on the floor. Then, she could arch her back like a cat. She can even meow if she wants!

Once she has practiced her animal stretches, ask her to show them to a family audience. Can your family members guess the animals she chose?

Number "Show-How"

Let your child show how well he knows numbers! Begin by saying a number. Have your child try to bend and stretch into that number's shape. For number one, he might stand on his toes and straighten his arms overhead.

To demonstrate more difficult numbers, such as two, he will have to be creative and flexible. He may curve his arms and kneel on the floor. In some cases, he may have to give a verbal description as well.

Later, allow him to show off his number "show-how" to a family audience and ask them to guess or even match his stretchy numbers.

* See page ii.

Character Development Activities

Taking Turns

Help your child make a book about taking turns. Fold 3-4 sheets of blank paper in half and staple the sheets along the fold. Title the book *I Take Turns!* and allow your child to decorate the cover.

Ask your child to draw pictures of how she takes turns during a day or week. For example, your child could draw a picture of herself waiting for a turn to drink from a water fountain. Once your child has filled the pages of her book, invite her to share her pictures and explain how each one shows that she is taking turns.

The Three Rs of Respect

Discuss with your child what it means to respect something using examples to which he can relate. Explain how important it is for your child to be considerate of another person's feelings, possessions, and ideas.

Introduce the three Rs of respect: respect for oneself, respect for others, and respect for Earth. Talk about how he can show respect for each. Then, help him make a list of actions he can take this summer to show his respect for the above. Post the list in a visible location to serve as a convenient respect reminder.

Respect Myself—I can eat healthy food.
I can exercise with Mom.
Respect Others—I can knock on the door to Thad's room.
I can feed Charlie his doggie dinner on time.
Respect Earth—I can turn off the water while I'm brushing my teeth.
I can recycle paper, cans, and plastic bottles.

Outdoor Extension Activities

Take It Outside!

Play "I See Shapes" outside. Find a comfortable place to sit with your child. In this game, the first player must find something that is a distinct shape and start the game by naming the shape. For example, you might see a trampoline and say, "I see a circle." Then, describe the object in a variety of ways, such as by color and size. Play until you have tested your child's knowledge of several shapes. Then, allow him to find and name different shapes and describe the objects to you.

Grab your gardening gloves and play in the dirt! Find a sandy or dusty area. Invite your child to use her finger to practice drawing shapes, numbers, and letters in the sand or dirt. Join your child by drawing your own shapes, letters, and numbers. Then, quiz her knowledge of these key concepts. You can also take turns drawing pictures to use as story starters. For example, draw a turtle and an umbrella. Have your child tell you a story about your drawings. Then, have your child draw two pictures for you to use in a story and talk about that story together.

Go on a number hike! As you hike, challenge your child to count groups of things. How many ladybugs are on that leaf? How many cars are parked on the block? Do you see more big dogs or more small dogs? Are there fewer mailboxes with the flags up than down? Look for opportunities throughout the summer to help your child notice numbers. Whether it is the prices on a menu or the distance on a highway sign, show your child how important numbers are in his growing world.

* See page ii.

Monthly Goals

Think of three goals that you would like to set for yourself this month. For example, you may want to spend extra time reading with your family. Have an adult help you write your goals on the lines.

Place a sticker next to each of your goals that you complete. Feel proud that you have met your goals!

1. _____ [PLACE STICKER HERE]

2. _____ [PLACE STICKER HERE]

3. _____ [PLACE STICKER HERE]

Word List

The following words are used in this section. They are good words for you to know. Read each word aloud with an adult. When you see a word from this list on a page, circle it with your favorite color of crayon.

black	orange
blue	purple
brown	red
green	set
many	yellow

SECTION II

Introduction to Strength

At the end of this section are fitness and character development activities that focus on strength. These activities are designed to get your child moving and thinking about strengthening his body and his character. Complete these activities throughout the month as time allows. If your child has limited mobility, feel free to modify any suggested exercises to fit their individual abilities.

Physical Strength

Like flexibility, strength is necessary for a child to be healthy. Children might think being strong means lifting an enormous amount of weight. However, strength is more than the ability to pick up heavy barbells. Explain that strength is built over time and point out to your child how much stronger he has become since he was a toddler. At that time, he could walk down the sidewalk. Now, he can run across a baseball field.

There are many opportunities for children to gain strength. Your child can carry grocery bags to build muscle in his arms and ride a bicycle to develop strength in his legs. Classic exercises such as push-ups and chin-ups are also fantastic strength builders.

Help your child set realistic, achievable goals to improve his physical strength based on the activities that he enjoys. Over the summer months, offer encouragement and praise as your child accomplishes his strength goals.

Strength of Character

As your child is building his physical strength, guide him to work on his inner strength as well. Explain that having strong character means standing up for his values, even if others do not agree with his viewpoint. Tell him that it is not always easy to show inner strength. Discuss real-life examples, such as a time that he was teased by another child at the playground. How did he use his inner strength to handle this situation?

Remind your child that inner strength can be shown in many ways. For example, your child can show strength by being honest, standing up for someone who needs help, and putting his best efforts into every task. Use your time together over the summer to help your child develop a strong sense of self, both physically and emotionally. Look for moments to acknowledge when he has demonstrated strength of character so that he can see his positive growth on the inside as well as on the outside.

Numbers & Counting

DAY 1

Count 11 baseballs.

Color 11 caps.

DAY 1

Numbers & Counting

Count the objects in each set. Circle the number that tells how many.

10   11

10   11

10   11

10   11

Numbers & Counting

DAY 2

Count 12 moons.

Color 12 stars.

DAY 2

Colors

Color the pictures red.

strawberry

stop sign

cherries

apple

Handwriting/Phonics

DAY 3

apple

Trace and write each letter.

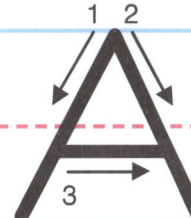

Circle the pictures that begin like .

dog

rainbow

astronaut

alligator

ant

53

© Carson Dellosa Education

DAY 3

Colors

Color the pictures orange.

pumpkin

carrot

fish

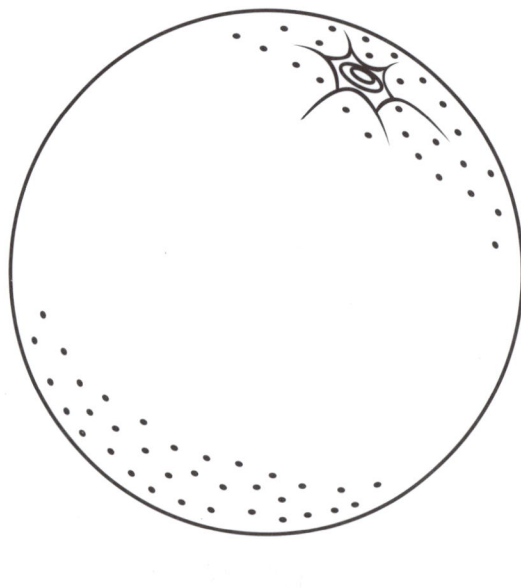
orange

Handwriting/Phonics

DAY 4

  balloon

Trace and write each letter.

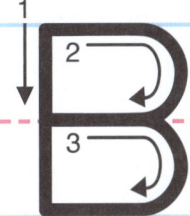

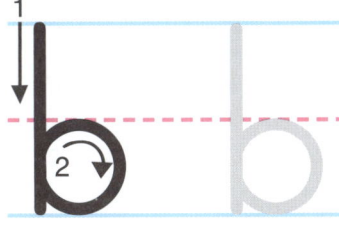

Circle the pictures that begin like .

bird

ball

sock

bee

horse

55

DAY 4

Colors

Color the pictures yellow.

sun

chick

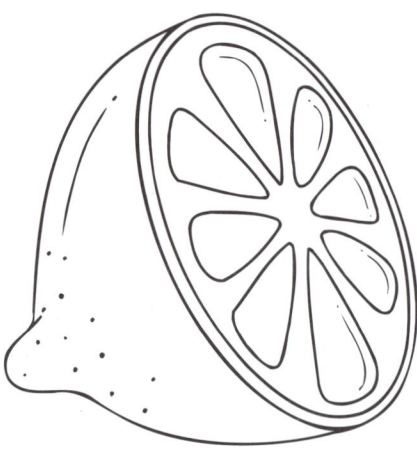
lemon

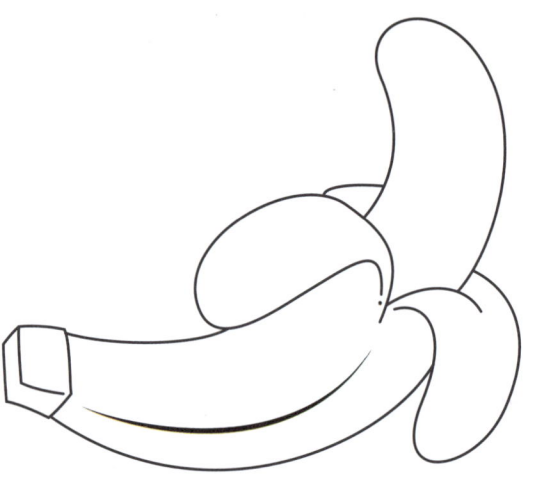
banana

Handwriting/Phonics

DAY 5

cake

Trace and write each letter.

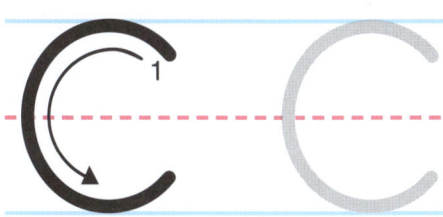

Circle the pictures that begin like .

net

zipper

car

carrot

cat

DAY 5

Colors

Color the pictures green.

tree

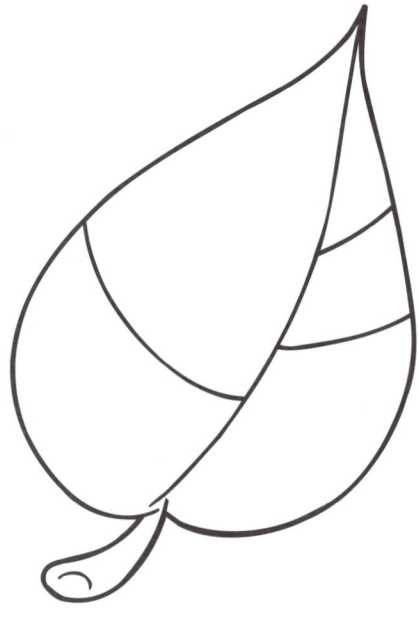

leaf

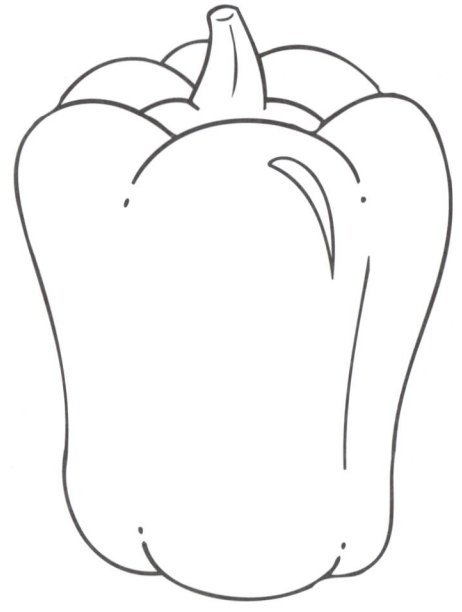

pepper

frog

Handwriting/Phonics

DAY 6

Dd

dog

Trace and write each letter.

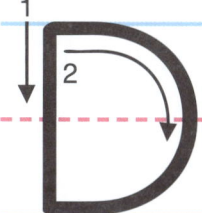

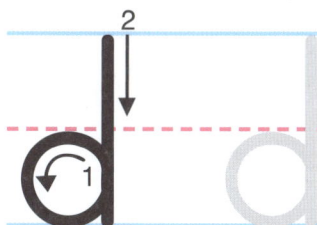

Circle the pictures that begin like .

desk

fish

jar

doll   duck

59

© Carson Dellosa Education

DAY 6

Colors

Color the pictures blue.

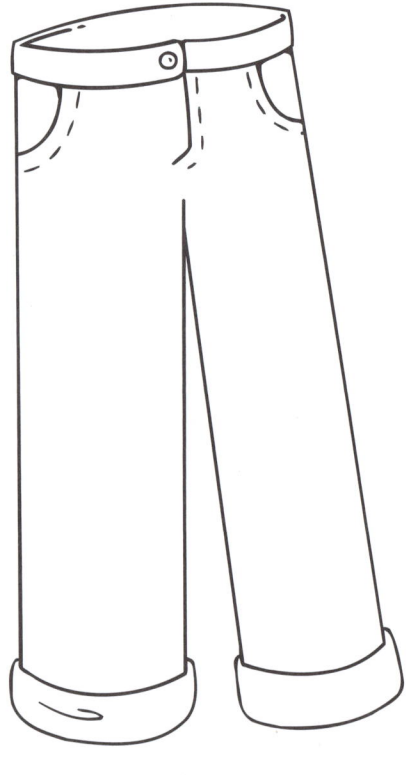
jeans

bluebird

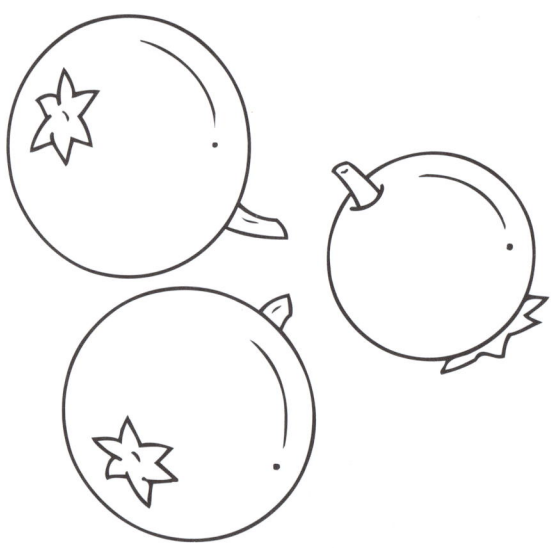
blueberries

ribbon

Handwriting/Phonics

DAY 7

egg

Trace and write each letter.

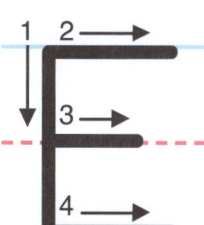

Circle the pictures that begin like .

eggplant

violin

envelope

banana

elephant

61
© Carson Dellosa Education

DAY 7

Colors

Color the pictures purple.

grapes

pansy

plum

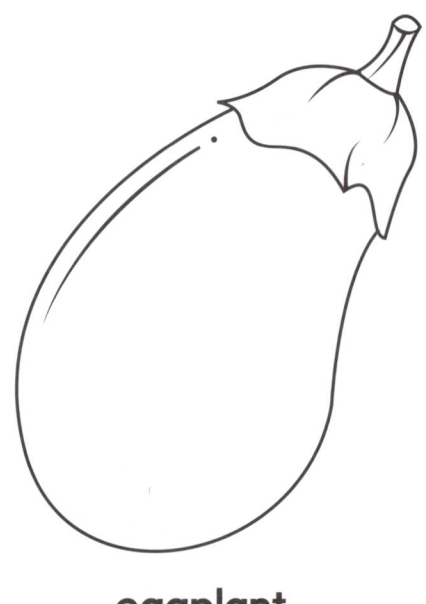

eggplant

Handwriting/Phonics

DAY 8

  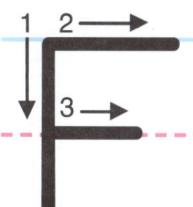

Trace and write each letter.

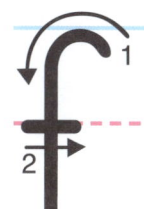

Circle the pictures that begin like .

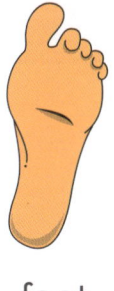
foot

fan

ball

feather

sun

63

© Carson Dellosa Education

DAY 8

Colors

Color the pictures black.

tire

bear

top hat

crow

Handwriting/Phonics

DAY 9

Gg

guitar

Trace and write each letter.

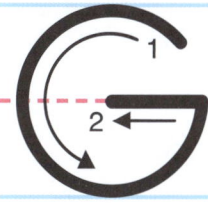 G

g

Circle the pictures that begin like .

gift

turtle

can

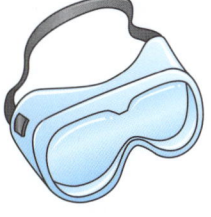
goggles

goat

65

DAY 9

Colors

Color the pictures brown.

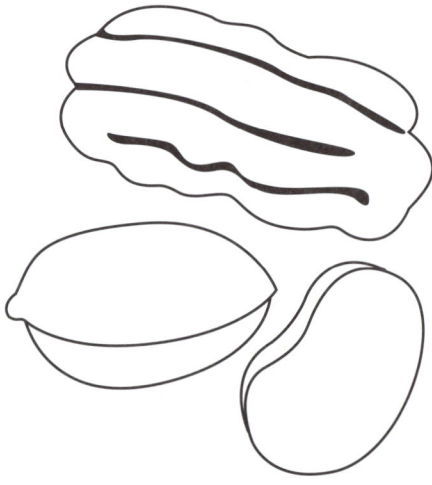

nuts

teddy bear

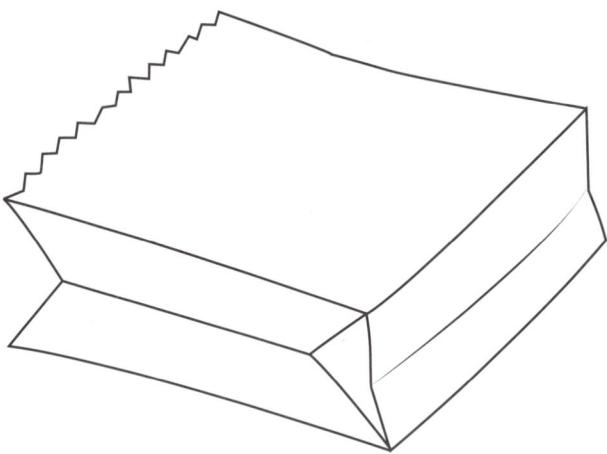

paper bag

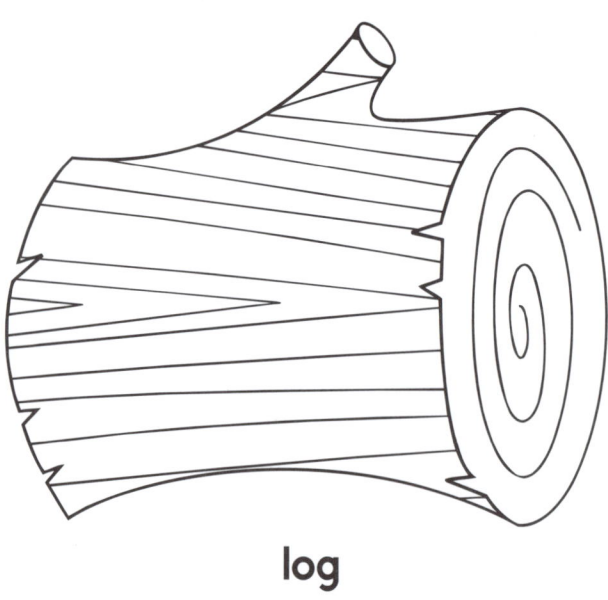

log

Handwriting/Phonics

DAY 10

  horse

Trace and write each letter.

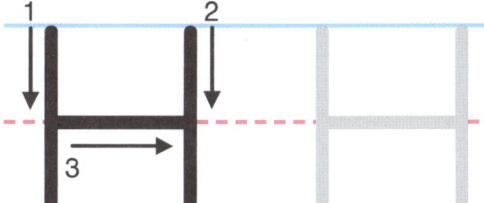

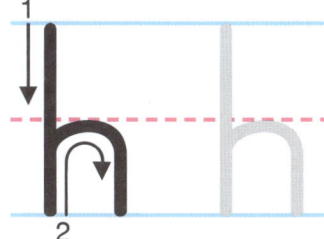

Circle the pictures that begin like .

hammer

hat

house

apple

fork

DAY 10

Numbers & Counting

Count the objects in each set. Circle the number that tells how many objects are shown.

3   4   5

3   4   5

2   3   4

4   5   6

3   4   5

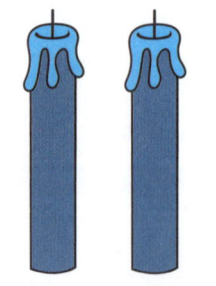 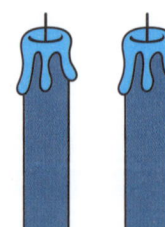 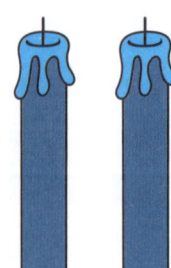

5   6   7

Handwriting/Phonics

DAY 11

igloo

Trace and write each letter.

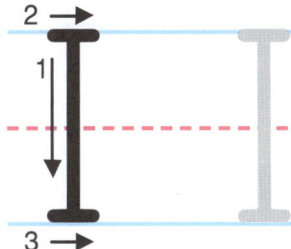

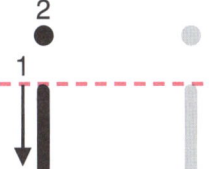

Circle the pictures that begin like .

iguana

duck

inch

lock

ink

69

DAY 11

Numbers & Counting

Count the objects in each set. Circle the number that tells how many.

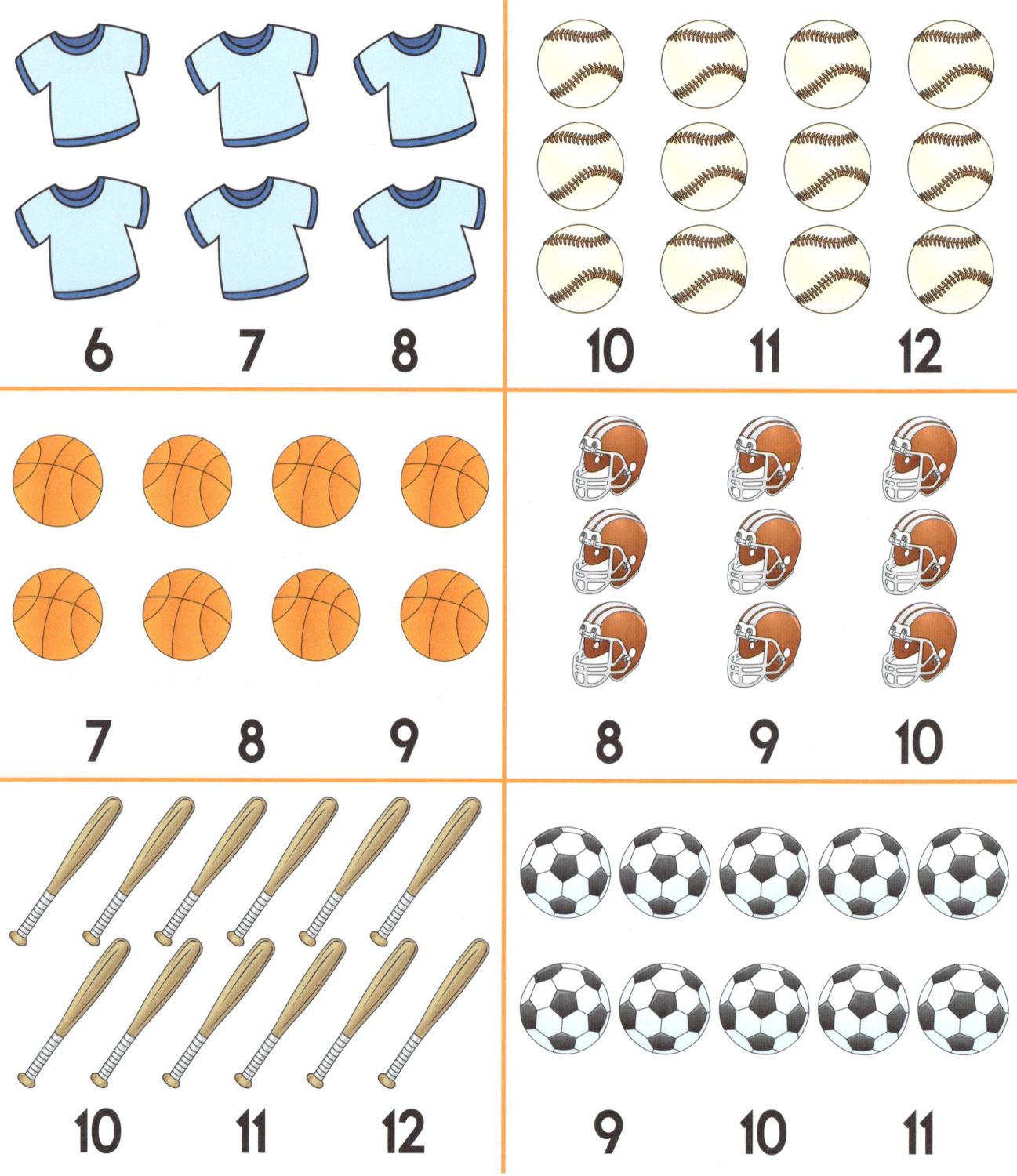

Handwriting/Phonics

DAY 12

  jar

Trace and write each letter.

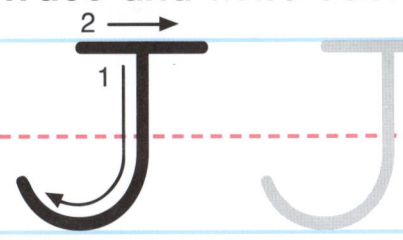

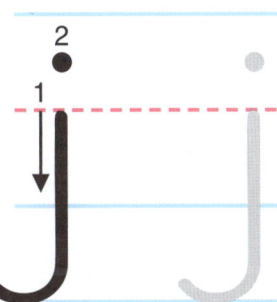

Circle the pictures that begin like .

jack-in-the-box

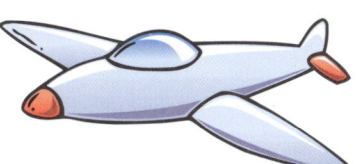

jet

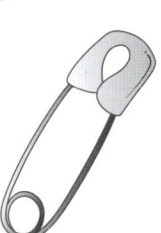

goat

jelly beans

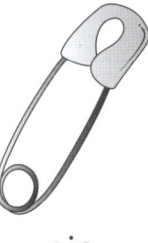

pin

71

DAY 12

Colors

Color each picture.

red

orange

yellow

green

blue

purple

black

brown

Handwriting/Phonics

DAY 13

  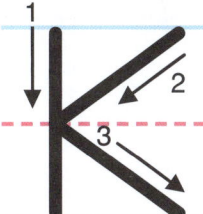

king

Trace and write each letter.

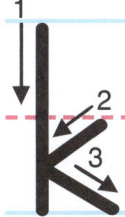

Circle the pictures that begin like .

keys

kangaroo

kite

tiger

pencil

73

DAY 13

Phonics

Say the name of each picture. Circle the letter that matches the beginning sound.

Example:

a ⓑ l

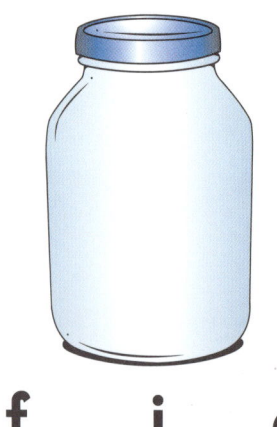

f j d

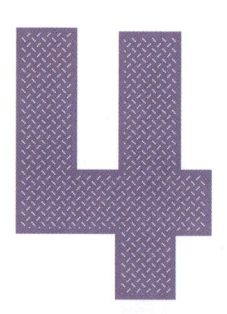

f d i

c e b

j c h

g a k

m i c

d k j

g h l

Handwriting/Phonics

DAY 14

 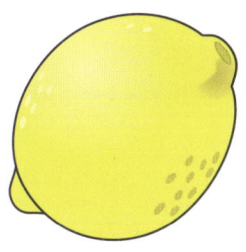 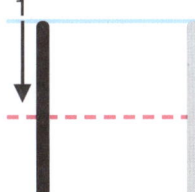 lemon

Trace and write each letter.

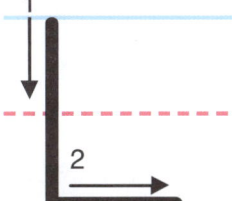

Circle the pictures that begin like .

lamp

hammer

book

lion

leaf

75

© Carson Dellosa Education

DAY 14

Numbers & Counting

Write the next numbers in each set.

1. | 4 | 5 |  |  |

2. | 12 | 13 | | |

Omar saw 4 dogs, 1 bird, 5 cats, and 2 fish at the pet store today. Color the graph to show the number of each animal that he saw.

Animals at the Pet Store

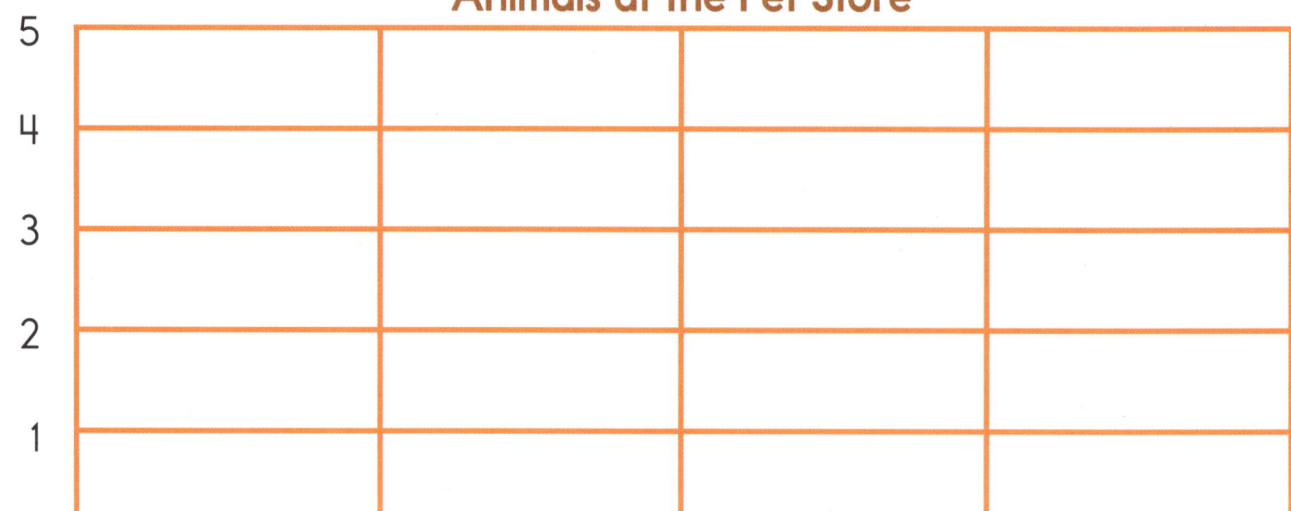

3. Omar saw more _____ than any other animal.

Handwriting/Phonics

DAY 15

 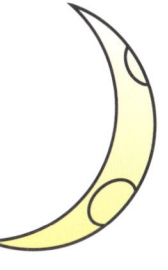 moon

Trace and write each letter.

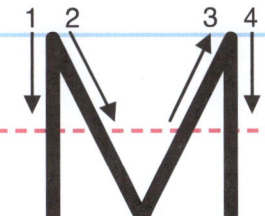

m

Circle the pictures that begin like 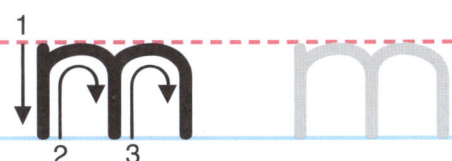.

mop

kite

tree

mitten

mouse

77

DAY 15

Visual Discrimination/Measurement

Circle the largest object in each group.

1.

2.

Circle the smallest object in each group.

3.

4.

Circle the object in each group that holds more.

5.

6.

Circle the object in each group that holds less.

7.

8.

Handwriting/Phonics

DAY 16

 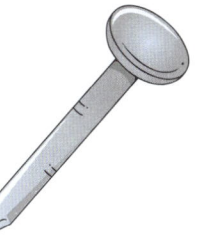

nail

Trace and write each letter.

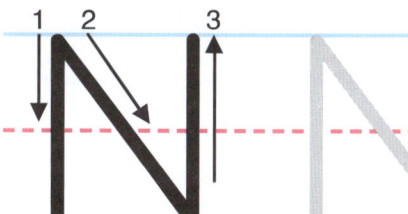

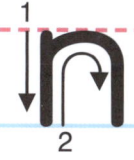

Circle the pictures that begin like .

nuts

carrot

lemon

nest

net

79

© Carson Dellosa Education

DAY 16

Describe each picture. Then, draw a line from each picture to a word that tells where something is.

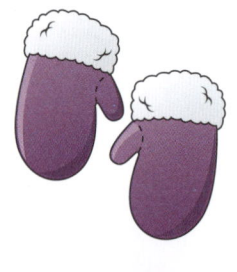   under

   in

   beside

   on

   above

Handwriting/Phonics

DAY 17

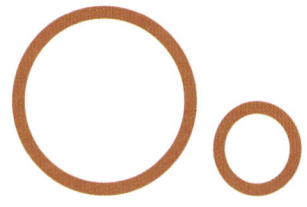  ostrich

Trace and write each letter.

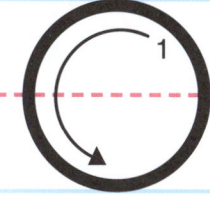

Circle the pictures that begin like .

bone

olive

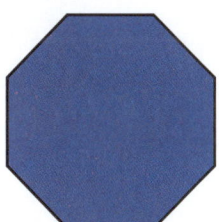

octagon

octopus

wagon

81

DAY 17

Shape Recognition/Colors

Use the key to color each shape.

◇ = red   □ = purple   △ = orange
▭ = blue   ○ = yellow   ⬭ = green

Handwriting/Phonics

DAY 18

  pumpkin

Trace and write each letter.

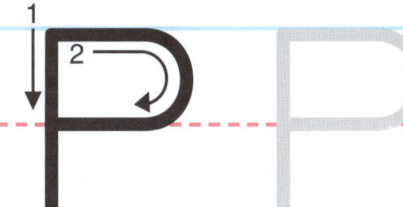

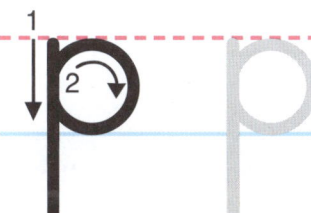

Circle the pictures that begin like .

yarn   igloo   pear   penguin   pie

DAY 18

Classification

Circle the living things.

Handwriting/Phonics

DAY 19

Qq  queen

Trace and write each letter.

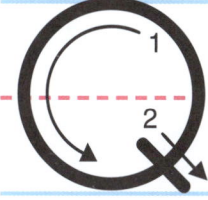

Circle the pictures that begin like .

yo-yo

quilt

quarter

ant

quail

85

© Carson Dellosa Education

DAY 19

Visual Discrimination

Draw a line to match each card to the envelope with the same shape and size.

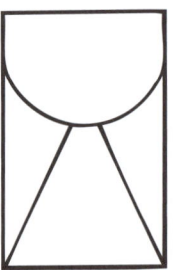

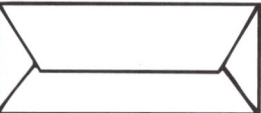

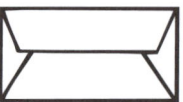

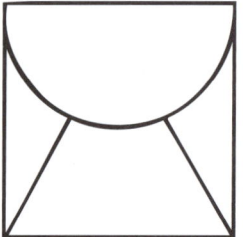

Handwriting/Phonics

DAY 20

  rocket

Trace and write each letter.

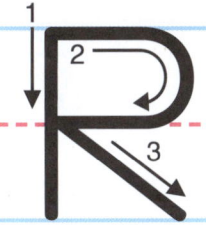

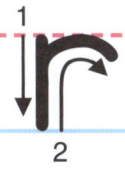

Circle the pictures that begin like .

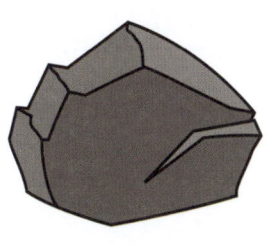
rock

ring

rabbit

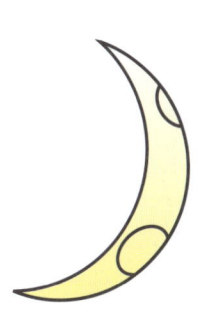
moon

giraffe

87

© Carson Dellosa Education

DAY 20

Visual Discrimination

Circle the uppercase letters in each set that are the same.

Example:

(F) E (F) B (F) A	P R R R H D	W W V W Y W
G O G G Y C	E D X D D L	H H H Y H Z
O Q G Q Q C	N M N N N Z	L F T C T T

88

Science Experiment

Absorbing Water

Which substances absorb the most water?

Materials:
- eyedropper
- scissors
- cup of water
- cardboard egg carton
- spoon

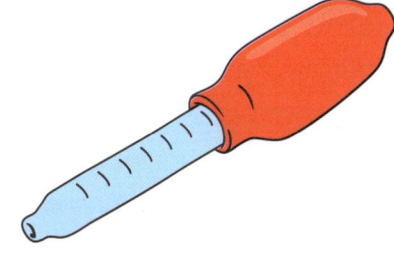

Substances:
- paper towel
- sponge
- toilet paper
- dirt
- aluminum foil
- newspaper
- waxed paper
- cotton ball
- cloth
- sand
- construction paper

Procedure: Help your child place a small amount of each substance into a separate section of the egg carton. Use the spoon to place the dirt and sand into the egg carton. Use the eyedropper to slowly add 5–10 drops of water to each section. Add the same amount of water to each substance. Observe whether the substance absorbed or did not absorb the water. Ask your child the questions below.

1. Which substances absorbed water? _____

2. Which substances did not absorb water? _____

3. Which substance absorbed the most water? _____

4. In this experiment, what does the word *substance* mean? Can you think of another substance you could use? _____

Fitness Activities

Push-Up Pick-Me-Up

Show your child how to do a push-up. Talk about how much upper body strength a push-up takes and let her try to complete one. If she is successful, have her attempt to do another. If she has trouble completing one push-up, celebrate her effort and talk about how difficult this exercise can be (especially if you had trouble doing it). Then, help her complete a modified push-up with her knees bent and her feet on the ground. After she has completed a few push-ups successfully, challenge her to complete as many push-ups as she can. Remind her to keep her back straight. Encourage her to continue doing sets of push-ups several times a week. At the end of the summer, see how many sets your child can complete. Discuss any demonstrated improvements with your child.

Wall Sits

Have your child stand straight against a wall. Ask him to bring his legs out in front of him. Next, he should bend his knees and slide down the wall until he is in a sitting position. Now, have him stand up and "sit" as many times as he can. Let him practice this every day for one week. Write how many wall sits he completes next to each day below. What does your child notice as his legs get stronger?

Sunday _____   Monday _____

Tuesday _____   Wednesday _____

Thursday _____   Friday _____

Saturday _____

* See page ii.

"Tug-of-Peace"

Get your family or neighbors involved in a friendly game of tug-of-war. Use a strong rope, or tie several sturdy pieces of fabric together. Mark the midpoint with a brightly colored scarf and place a straight marker, such as a ruler, on the ground.

For the first round, assign unequal teams by placing the strongest players, or more players, on one team. After the team with the unfair advantage wins, ask your child to tell you why she thinks that team won. Then, discuss what it means to be fair using examples to which she can relate, such as treating others the way she wants to be treated.

Then, help your child reassign teams so that the game is played more fairly. Celebrate as a group by having a summer snack, such as watermelon, cut into fair, equal portions!

Invitation to Integrity

Discuss with your child what it means to have integrity using examples to which he can relate, such as standing up for what he believes in. Then, appoint a time to hold a family meeting to talk about your family's values. This meeting should include a discussion about the standards and rules your family lives by or will agree to live by.

Next, provide your child with craft materials and have him create an invitation to the family meeting for each family member. Make sure he includes the time, date, and place to meet. Have him deliver the invitations or present them during a family time, such as breakfast or dinner.

Involve your child as much as possible during the meeting. Use poster board and a marker to list your family's key beliefs in simple language. After the meeting, post the list in a visible location as a positive reminder of what integrity means to your family.

* See page ii.

Outdoor Extension Activities

Take It Outside!

Clean up your neighborhood with your child. Put on protective clothing and gloves, and get two heavy-duty trash bags so that you and your child can pick up litter outside your home, at a park, or along the beach. As you are practicing the character trait of respect for Earth, use this time to talk about the importance of taking care of the world around you. Listen to your child's ideas and let him brainstorm possibilities for making Earth a better place to live.

Make a fun outdoor treasure hunt with an alphabet twist. Have your child write the letters of the alphabet along the left side of a sheet of paper. Invite her to take her letter list and a pencil outside to search for outdoor objects that begin with each letter of the alphabet. For challenging letters, such as *q* and *x*, be more flexible by helping her to record a *quiet butterfly* or an *extra flower*. When you get home, ask your child to draw a picture that tells about the treasure hunt. Have your child dictate a caption for you to write that goes with the drawing.

Summer is the perfect time to start a collection. Whether your child is interested in rocks, leaves, or another item found in nature, encourage him to collect a variety of the objects. Provide him with a container to gather his treasures. Once he has found several items, have him organize them into groups based on similarities. For example, he could group the objects by color, shape, or size. When his collection is complete, help him find a way to decorate and display his objects.

* See page ii.

SECTION III

Monthly Goals

Think of three goals that you would like to set for yourself this month. For example, you may want to learn three new words each week. Have an adult help you write your goals on the lines.

Place a sticker next to each of your goals that you complete. Feel proud that you have met your goals!

1. _____ PLACE STICKER HERE

2. _____ PLACE STICKER HERE

3. _____ PLACE STICKER HERE

Word List

The following words are used in this section. They are good words for you to know. Read each word aloud with an adult. When you see a word from this list on a page, circle it with your favorite color of crayon.

add	more
box	name
fewer	number
find	order
letter	word

SECTION III

Introduction to Endurance

At the end of this section are fitness and character development activities that focus on endurance. These activities are designed to get your child moving and thinking about developing her physical and mental stamina. Complete these activities throughout the month as time allows. If your child has limited mobility, feel free to modify any suggested exercises to fit their individual abilities.

Physical Endurance

Many children seem to have endless energy and can run, jump, and play for hours. But, other children may not have that kind of endurance. Improving endurance requires regular aerobic exercise, which causes the heart to beat faster and the person to breathe harder. Regular aerobic activity makes the heart grow stronger and the blood cells deliver oxygen to the body more efficiently. There are many ways for a child to get an aerobic workout that does not feel like exercise. Jumping rope and playing tag are examples.

If you see your child head for the TV, suggest an activity that will get her moving instead. Explain that while there are times when a relaxing activity is valuable, it is important to take advantage of the warm mornings and sunny days to go outdoors. Leave the less active times for when it is dark, too hot, or raining. Explain the importance of physical activity and invite her to join you for a walk, a bicycle ride, or a game of basketball.

Endurance and Character Development

Endurance applies to the mind as well as to the body. Explain to your child that *endurance* means to stick with something. Children can demonstrate mental endurance every day. For example, staying with a task when she might want to quit and keeping at it until it is complete are ways that a child can show endurance.

Help your child practice her mental endurance. Look for situations where she might seem frustrated or bored. Perhaps she asked to take swimming lessons, but after a few early morning classes, she is not having as much fun as she imagined. Turn this dilemma into a learning tool. It is important that children feel some ownership in decision making, so guide her to some key points to consider, such as how she asked to take lessons. Remind her that she has taken only a few lessons, so she might become more used to the early mornings. Let her know that she has options to make the experience more enjoyable, such as going to bed earlier or sleeping a few extra minutes during the morning car ride. Explain that quitting should be the last resort. Teaching your child to endure will help her as she continues to develop into a happy, healthy person.

Handwriting/Phonics

DAY 1

Ss

sun

Trace and write each letter.

Circle the pictures that begin like .

sandwich

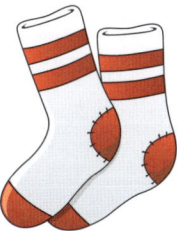
socks

soap

keys

pear

95

DAY 1

Classification/Phonics

Circle the things that are not living.

butterfly

balloon

mug

penguin

book

house

Circle the two pictures in each row with names that rhyme.

Handwriting/Phonics

DAY 2

  turtle

Trace and write each letter.

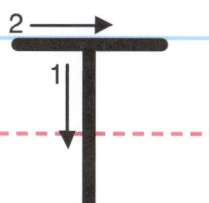

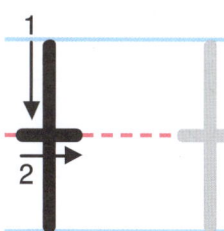

Circle the pictures that begin like .

teddy bear   tent   turkey

net   hand

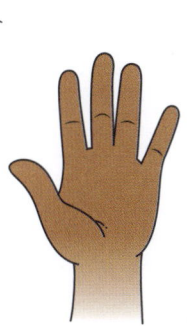
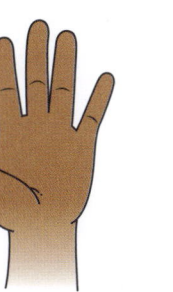

97

DAY 2

Visual Discrimination

Circle the lowercase letters in each set that are the same.

Example:

(e) f i	p d o	c s o
(e)(e) p	d n d	s s s
r n r	v v y	p d d
r b i	v d v	d b d
g p g	i j i	j g p
y g g	i n i	j j y

Handwriting/Phonics

DAY 3

  umbrella

Trace and write each letter.

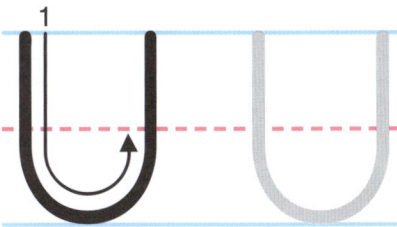

Circle the pictures that begin like .

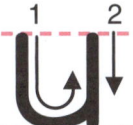 undershirt

 pumpkin

 under

 up

 egg

99

DAY 3

Phonics

Say the name of the thing in each picture. Clap once for each syllable in the word. Circle the number that tells how many syllables are in the word.

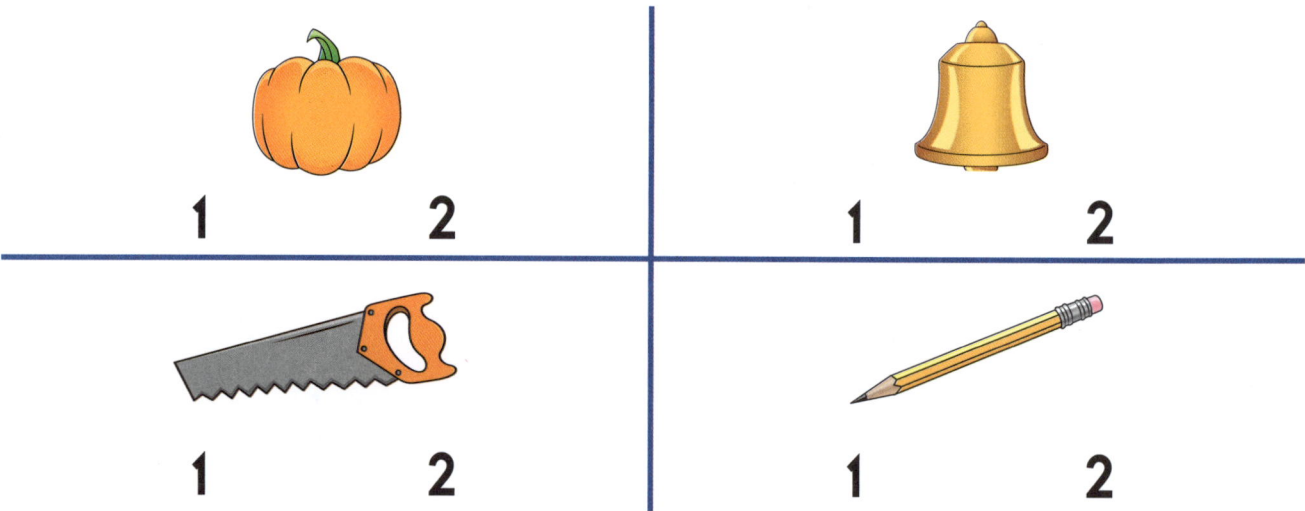

1 2	1 2
1 2	1 2

Each word below is written as two separate syllables. Write the whole word on the line. Blend the two syllables, and say the word out loud.

ti   ger

rain   bow

spi   der

100

© Carson Dellosa Education

PLACE STICKER HERE

Handwriting/Phonics

DAY 4

vase

Trace and write each letter.

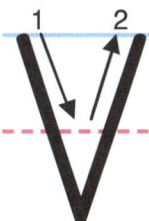

Circle the pictures that begin like .

van   vacuum   vest   yo-yo   banana

101

© Carson Dellosa Education

DAY 4

Grammar & Language Arts

Some words have more than one meaning. Read each sentence. Circle the picture that shows how the word in red is used.

The **bat** ate a bug.

The jet will **fly** over my house.

Ella can **park** the car.

Write the word from the box that completes each sentence.

| am   had   is |

Tess _____ first in line.

| My   I   By |

_____ like the red hat best.

| as   at   and |

Min _____ Sam swim in the pool.

Handwriting/Phonics

DAY 5

  window

Trace and write each letter.

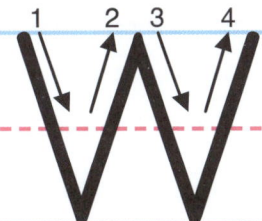

Circle the pictures that begin like .

mailbox

wagon

web

watch   jar

103
© Carson Dellosa Education

DAY 5

Numbers & Counting

Point to each number. Count to 100 by ones and by tens.

1	2	3	4	5	6	7	8	9	10
11	12	13	14	15	16	17	18	19	20
21	22	23	24	25	26	27	28	29	30
31	32	33	34	35	36	37	38	39	40
41	42	43	44	45	46	47	48	49	50
51	52	53	54	55	56	57	58	59	60
61	62	63	64	65	66	67	68	69	70
71	72	73	74	75	76	77	78	79	80
81	82	83	84	85	86	87	88	89	90
91	92	93	94	95	96	97	98	99	100

© Carson Dellosa Education

PLACE STICKER HERE

Handwriting/Phonics

DAY 6

 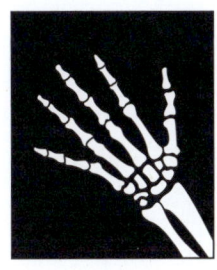 

Trace and write each letter.

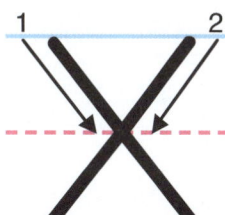

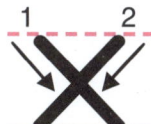

Circle the pictures that have the letter *x*, like .

box

queen

fox

ox

barn

105

© Carson Dellosa Education

Numbers & Counting

DAY 6

Count each kind of animal. Color one box for each animal that you find.

Handwriting/Phonics

DAY 7

Y y

Trace and write each letter.

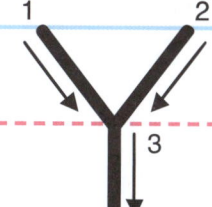

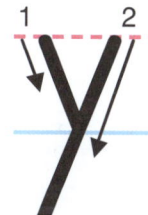

Circle the pictures that begin like .

yogurt

yo-yo

lemon

rabbit

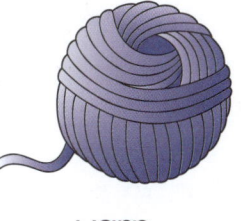
yarn

107

DAY 7

Numbers & Counting

Write the missing numbers.

1	----	----	----	----
6	----	----	----	----
11	----	----	14	----
----	----	----	19	----

Handwriting/Phonics

DAY 8

Zz

zigzag

Trace and write each letter.

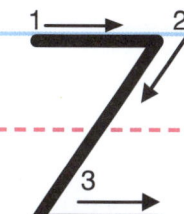

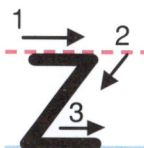

Circle the pictures that begin like 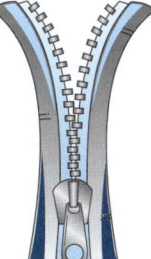 **.**

zipper

guitar

zebra

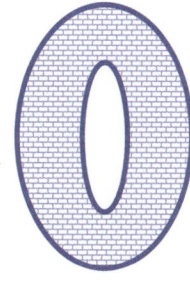
zero

seal

DAY 8

Numbers & Counting

Count how many items are in each group. Circle the number that is the same as the number of items.

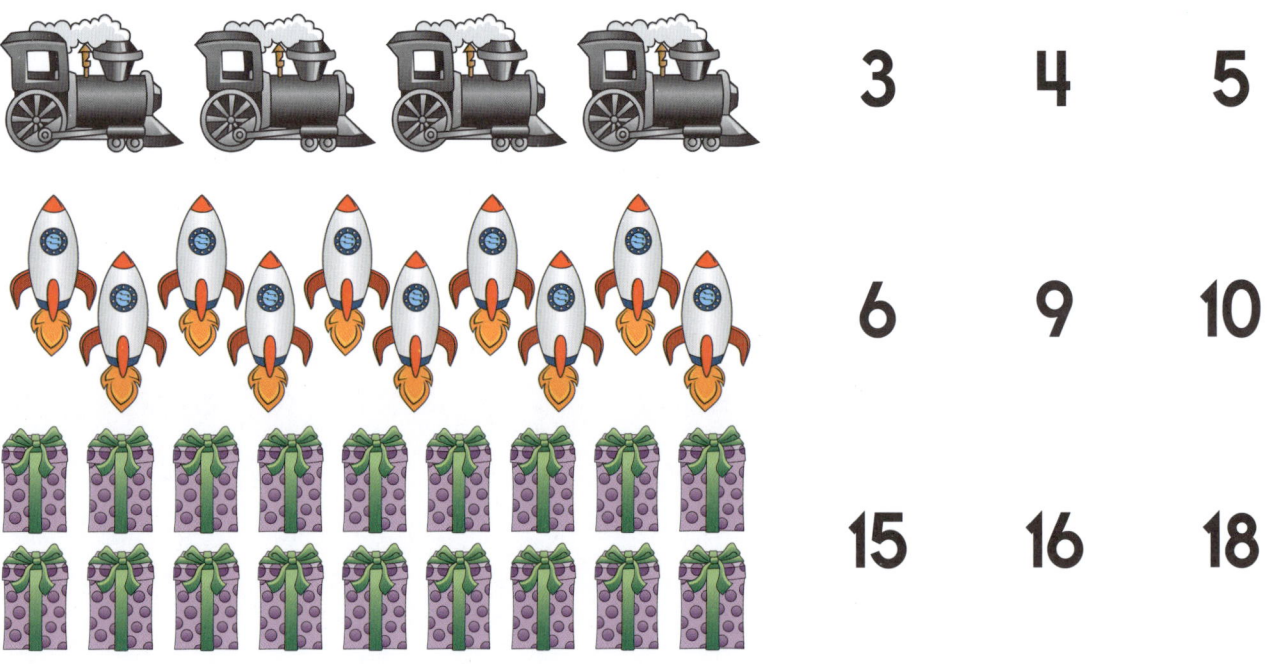

3	4	5
6	9	10
15	16	18

Circle the group that shows more oranges than apples.

Circle the group that shows fewer cats than rats.

Circle the group that shows the same number of eggs as nests.

Alphabet/Handwriting

DAY 9

Write the uppercase letters of the alphabet in order on the train cars. Circle each train car that has a letter from your first name.

DAY 9

Grammar & Language Arts

A *noun* is a word that names a person, a place, or a thing. Circle each person. Draw an X on each place. Draw a square around each thing.

baby	school	man

farm	sock	van

A *verb* is a word that shows an action. Circle the words and pictures that show verbs.

zebra	run	eat

wave	apple	hug

Numbers & Counting

DAY 10

In each space, write the number you can add to make 10.

1 +  = 10

7 +  = 10

4 +  = 10

5 + _____ = 10

DAY 10

Numbers & Counting

Look at the pictures. Complete the addition sentences.

2 + 3 = _____

2 + 2 = _____

Look at the pictures. Complete the subtraction sentences.

3 − 2 = _____

5 − 1 = _____

Classification

DAY 11

Circle the things you can see.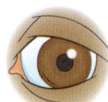

flowers

teddy bear

music

rainbow

car

Circle the things you can hear.

laughter

doorbell

bag

pear

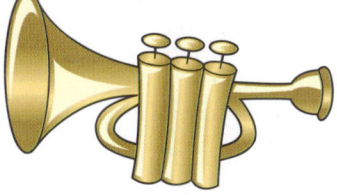
horn

115
© Carson Dellosa Education

DAY 11

Classification

Circle the things you can taste.

| ice-cream cone | sandwich | house | apple |

Circle the things you can smell.

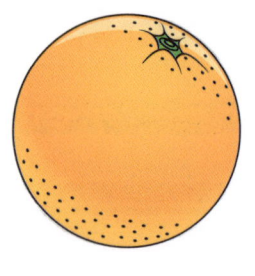 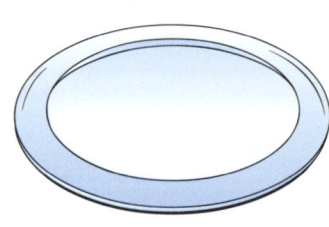  

| orange | plate | flower | bread |

Circle the things you can touch.

| cat | teddy bear | hat | moon |

Grammar & Language Arts/Measurement

DAY 12

Draw a line to match each word to its opposite.

up

smile

open

hot

closed

frown

cold

down

Which bird is heavier? Circle it.

Which bowl has more fish? Circle it.

Which is harder? Circle it.

DAY 12

Sequencing

Number the pictures in the order that they happened.

Visual Discrimination/Measurement

DAY 13

Circle the object in each set that has more.

  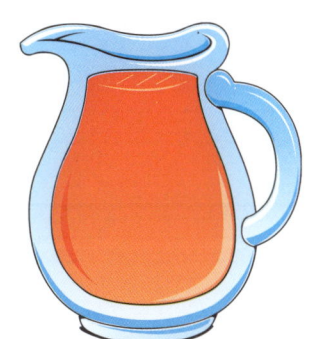 

DAY 13

Shape Recognition/Grammar & Language Arts

Match each solid shape to an object with a similar shape.

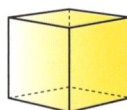

Fill in each blank with a question word from the box.

| What   When |

_____ is on her back?

_____ will it be time for dinner?

Phonics

DAY 14

Say the name of each picture. Circle the letter it begins with.

   a   b

   a   b

   b   c

   a   c

   a   c

DAY 14

Phonics

Say the name of each picture. Circle the letter it begins with.

　　e　　f

　　d　　e

　　d　　f

　　f　　d

　　d　　e

Phonics

DAY 15

Say the name of each picture. Circle the letter it begins with.

   i   g

   g   h

   h   i

   g   h

   i   g

DAY 15

Say the name of each picture. Circle the letter it begins with.

Phonics

DAY 16

Say the name of each picture. Circle the letter it begins with.

   m   o

   n   o

   m   n

   o   m

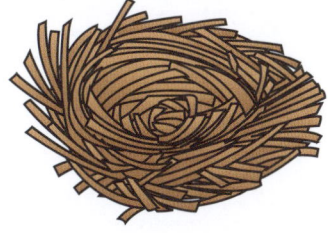   n   m

DAY 16

Phonics

Say the name of each picture. Circle the letter it begins with.

   p   r

   q   r

   r   p

   p   q

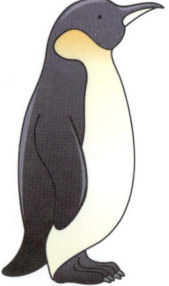   r   p

Phonics

DAY 17

Say the name of each picture. Circle the letter it begins with.

   s   t

   s   t

   t   s

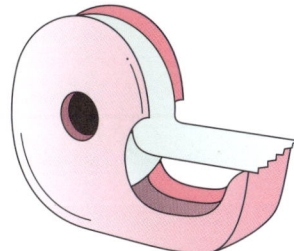   t   s

   s   t

DAY 17

Phonics

Say the name of each picture. Circle the letter it begins with.

u   v

w   u

w   v

u   w

v   u

Phonics

DAY 18

Say the name of each picture. Circle the letter it begins with.

   x   z

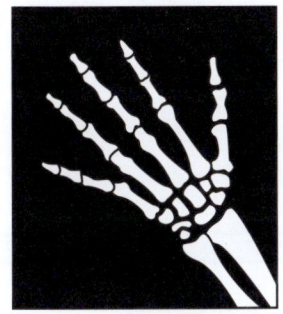   y   x

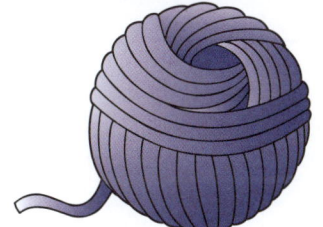   z   y

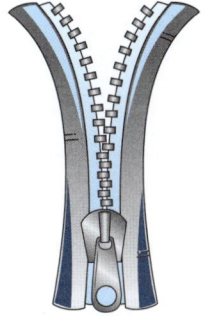   x   z

   y   x

DAY 18

Phonics

Say the name of each picture. Circle each picture whose name has the short *a* sound you hear in the middle of .

Say the name of each picture. Write the missing short *a*.

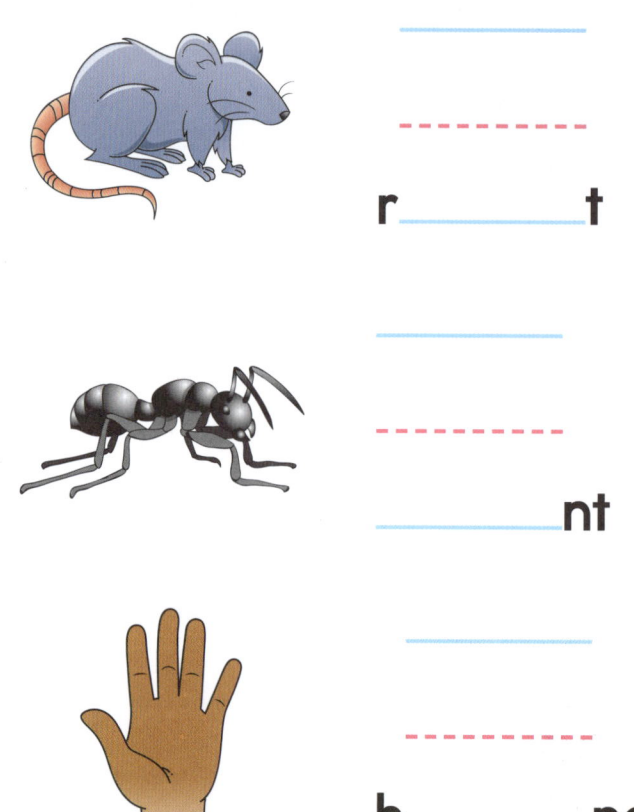

r____t

____nt

h____nd

Phonics

DAY 19

Say the name of each picture. Circle each picture whose name has the short *e* sound you hear in the middle of 🛏.

Say the name of each picture. Write the missing short *e*.

w_____b

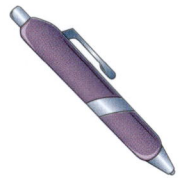

p_____n

h_____n

DAY 19

Say the name of each picture. Circle each picture whose name has the short *i* sound you hear in the middle of .

Say the name of each picture. Write the missing short *i*.

w____g

l____ps

b____b

Phonics

DAY 20

Say the name of each picture. Write the missing short o.

r____ck

m____p

l____ck

Say the name of each picture. Write the missing short u.

m____g

n____t

t____b

DAY 20

Measurement

Have an adult help you measure your height again. Fill in the blank. Compare this measurement to your measurement on page 3. Then, draw yourself below and color the picture.

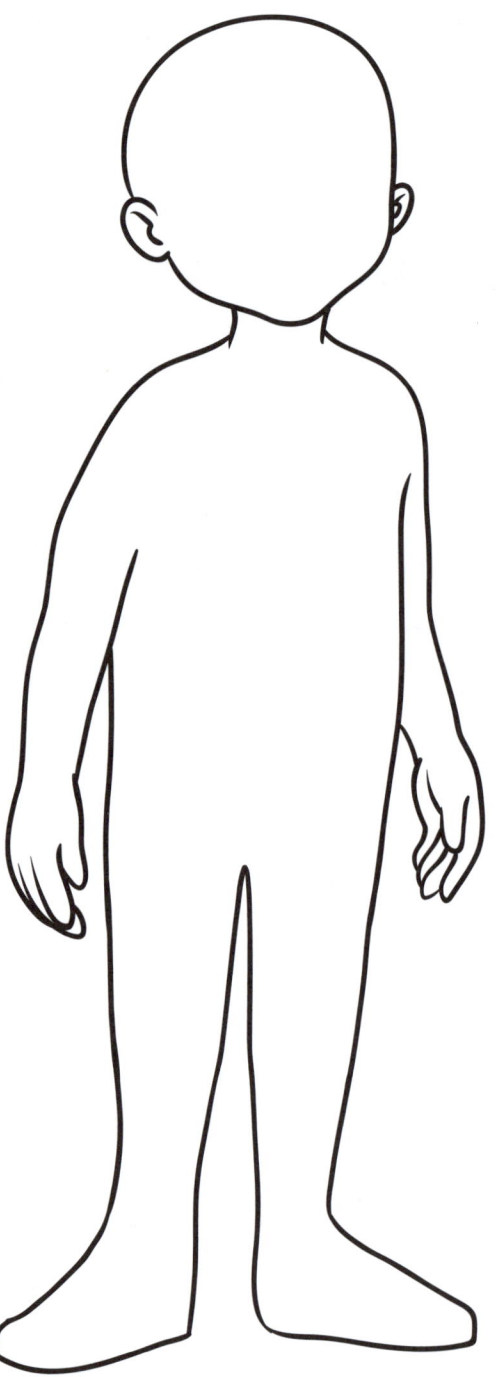

Your Height:

_____

Sun and Shade

Do objects in the sun feel warmer than objects in the shade? Which colors absorb the most heat?

Materials:
- 2 sheets of black paper
- 2 sheets of white paper

Procedure:
Help your child place one sheet of black paper and one sheet of white paper in direct sunlight. Place one sheet of black paper and one sheet of white paper in complete shade. After one hour, touch each sheet of paper. Compare the paper in the sun with the paper in the shade. Next, ask your child the following questions.

1. Which sheet of paper felt the warmest? _____

2. Which sheet of paper felt the coolest? _____

3. Why did one pair of papers feel warmer than the other pair? _____

4. What color shirt would keep you cooler on a sunny day? _____

Fitness Activities

Jumping Jack Challenge

Provide your child with an opportunity to show his endurance level and to challenge yours. Select short, fun, upbeat songs. Turn on the music and start doing jumping jacks along with your child. See if you both can jump through the first song together. Continue for a few songs and rest in between based on your and your child's stamina. If you find that jumping jacks are too challenging, simply jumping in place will also provide great exercise and an endurance challenge. Complete another jumping jack challenge each week. With each jumping jack session, incorporate longer songs and take fewer breaks to see how you both progress as your endurance improves.

Jump and Count

For this activity, you and your child will need the number flash cards at the back of this book and a jump rope.

Help your child shuffle the number flash cards and place them facedown on the ground. Flip over a number flash card. Your child should jump rope the number of times shown. Count your child's jumps aloud together. Once all of the cards have been flipped over, have your child arrange them in order from 0 to 12. Take turns jumping rope and flipping number flash cards until you have each completed the activity twice.

* See page ii.

Yes, I Can!

Explain to your child that perseverance means refusing to give up. Ask your child to draw a picture of the hardest thing she has ever done. Once she has finished, invite her to share her picture with you and tell you the story. Then, post her picture in a visible location as a reminder to never give up.

Supporting Stories

Discuss with your child what it means to be loyal using examples to which he can relate, such as supporting and standing up for the people in his life. Invite your child to write a story about loyalty. Talk about an example of loyalty that he has seen or experienced. Remind him of recent events if needed. Talk about how to turn this into a story. Have him recall the order of events as you record them on paper. His story should have a beginning, a middle, and an end.

Provide him with craft materials to make a book cover. Bind the book with staples or punch holes along the book's spine and secure it with brass paper fasteners or yarn. Help him add a title that incorporates the idea of loyalty.

Outdoor Extension Activities

Take It Outside!

Play a game of hopscotch to reinforce counting skills. Use sidewalk chalk to draw a basic, numbered hopscotch pattern on a safe sidewalk or driveway. Find two outdoor objects for you and your child to pick up, such as pinecones or smooth stones. To add counting and physical challenges, draw another hopscotch pattern with random numbers so that your child has to jump a little farther and find the numbers in order. Add more numbers as your child becomes familiar with each pattern.

Invite your child to a summer picnic! Make sandwiches, snacks, and drinks. Put it all in a picnic basket and grab a blanket. Before eating, talk about the five senses—taste, smell, sight, hearing, and touch. As your child eats each food item, talk about the variety of tastes and smells, such as the salty potato chips and sweet apple slices. Point out the things you and your child can hear, see, and feel during the picnic, like the crunch of the carrots, the color of the birds, and the softness of the grass beneath the blanket.

Explain to your child that when paper, plastic, metal, or glass is recycled, it is remade into something useful. For example, plastic milk jugs may become building materials. Recycled glass bottles or aluminum cans can be remade into new bottles or cans.

Talk about ways that recycling is good for the planet, such as conserving natural resources and saving landfill space. If your community participates in a recycling program, allow your child to help you sort the recyclable items or take a trip to the recycling center to drop off materials for recycling.

* See page ii.

Story Events

After you and your child have read several books from the suggested Summer Reading for Everyone list on pages viii–ix, ask your child to choose a favorite. Reread the book together. Then, have your child draw a picture illustrating an event from the book. Admire your child's drawing and ask her questions like these: What is happening in this part? Where does it happen? What characters are here? What do you like about this part of the story? Below or beside the picture, write what your child tells you about the story. Read the words together. Encourage your child to write any words she is comfortable with. Display the drawing and writing so that your child can tell other members of the family about the book.

Nonfiction Knowledge

Choose one of the nonfiction books from the Summer Reading List. Help your child find the names of the author and the illustrator on the cover of the book. Ask your child to explain what authors and illustrators do. Then, go through the book together, paying close attention to the illustrations. Ask your child how the illustrations match the text. Do they help you understand the words better? Do they provide additional information? Challenge your child to come up with a new illustration for one page of the book. He can make a drawing or painting, put together a collage, or take a photograph.

Tell It Again!

Ask your child to choose one of the fiction books you have read from the Summer Reading for Everyone list. Reread it together to refresh your child's memory. Then, ask her to retell the story to you or to a friend or family member. Encourage your child to include as many details as possible. Another option is to invite your child to act out scenes from the story. She can play the main character, and you (or a sibling or friend) can play a supporting role.

BONUS

Phonics

Match each word to the correct picture.

Example:

sun

dog

bat

pin

hen

Phonics

BONUS

Match each word to the correct picture.

gum

egg

nut

ant

log

BONUS

Phonics

Circle the word in each row that names the picture.

	cap	van	rat
	tip	job	sun
	day	boy	bed
	on	ant	end
	bat	yak	fun

Phonics

BONUS

Circle the word in each row that names the picture.

	cat	in	mug
	am	leg	up
	mop	bug	dip
	mat	net	hit
	rag	jet	wig

BONUS

Handwriting

Trace and write the letters A–E.

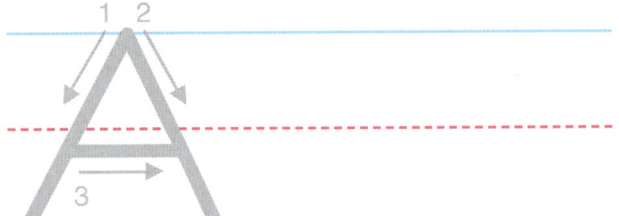 

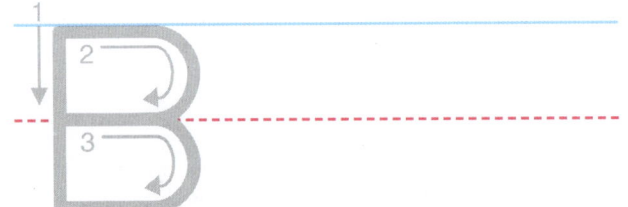 

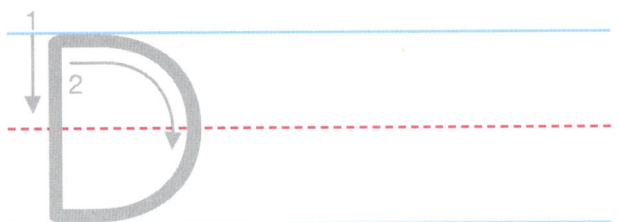 

Handwriting

BONUS

Trace and write the letters F–J.

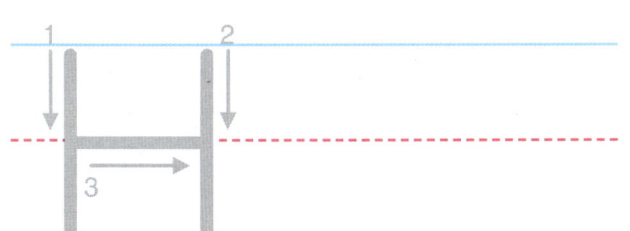
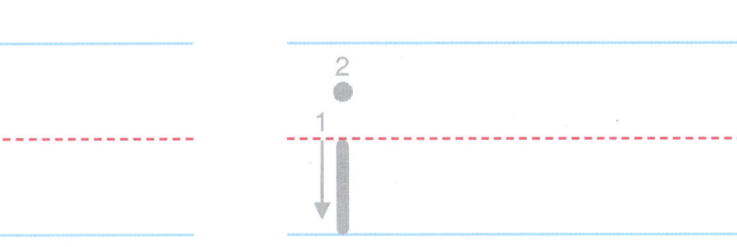
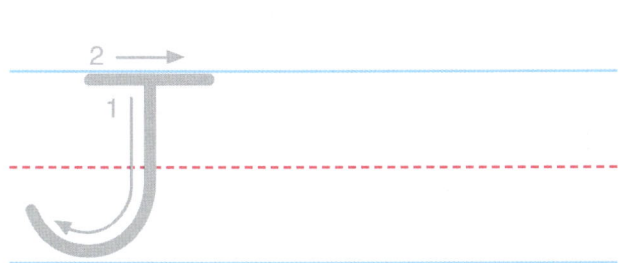

BONUS

Handwriting

Trace and write the letters K–O.

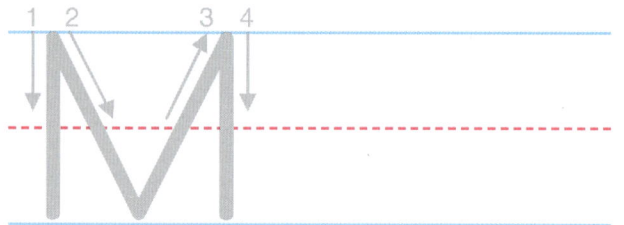 

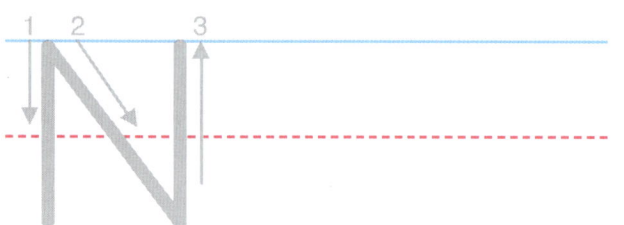 

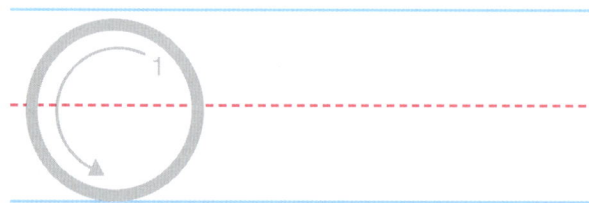 

Handwriting

BONUS

Trace and write the letters P–T.

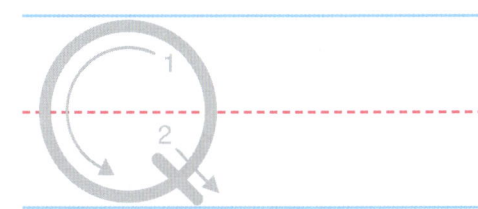

BONUS

Handwriting

Trace and write the letters U–Y.

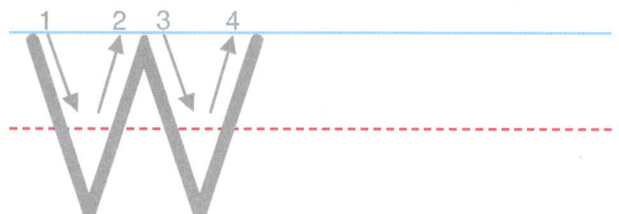

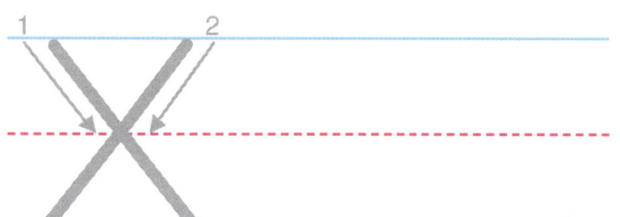

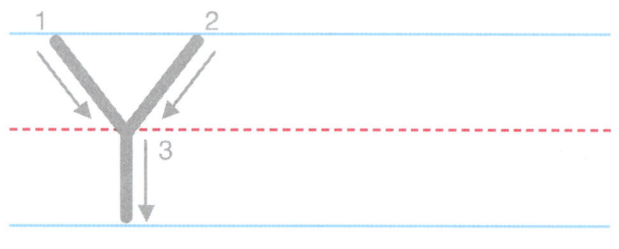

Handwriting

BONUS

Trace and write the letter Z.

Trace and write the numbers 0–5.

BONUS

Handwriting

Trace and write the numbers 6–10.

 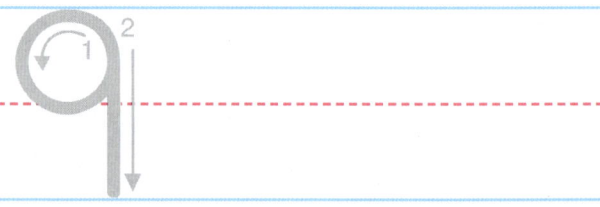

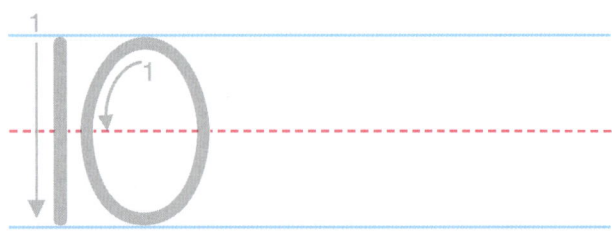

Practice writing your name.

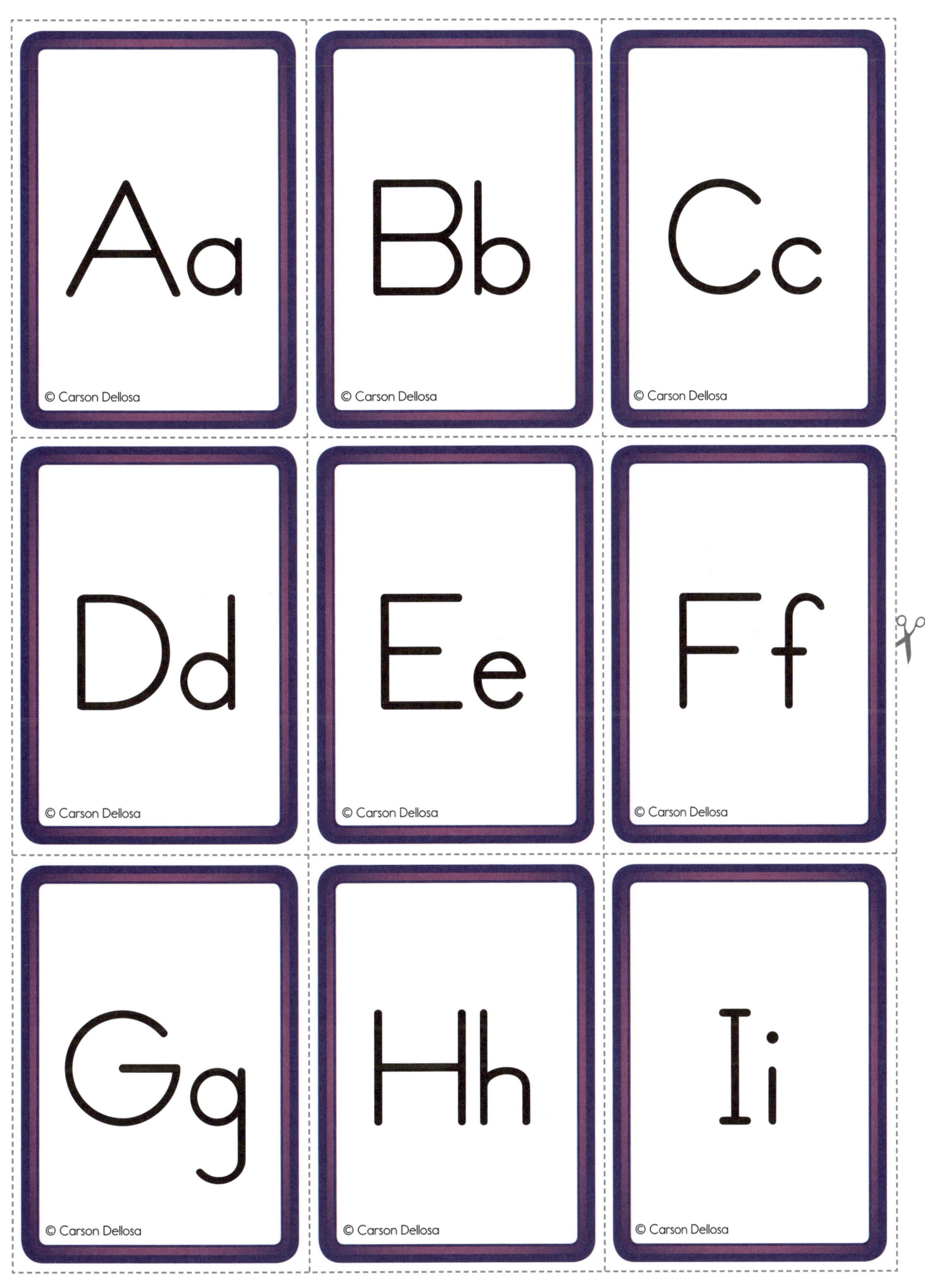

 car	 baseball bat	 apple
 feather	 elephant	 dog
 inch	 hammer	 goat

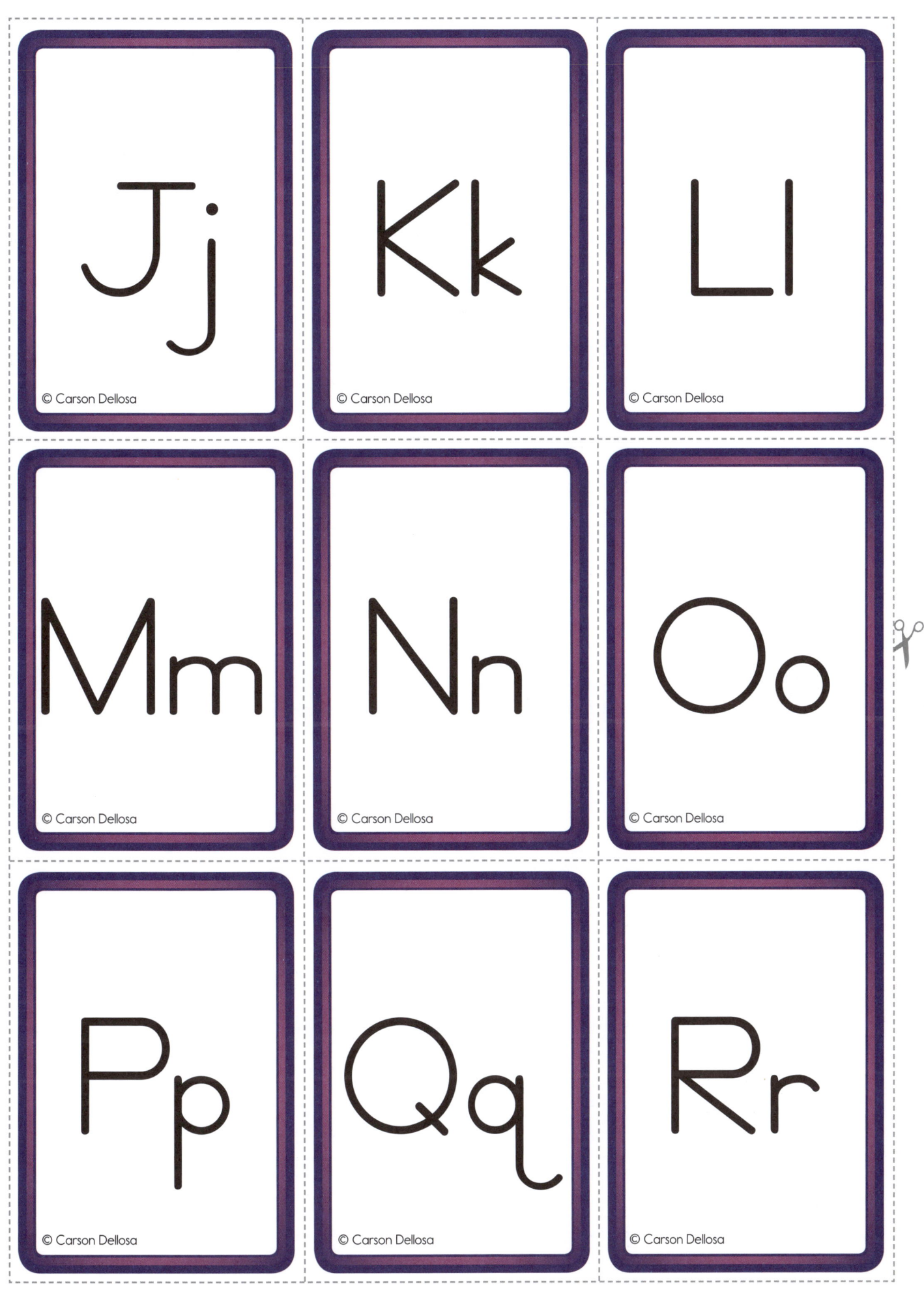

leaf

kangaroo

jack-in-the-box

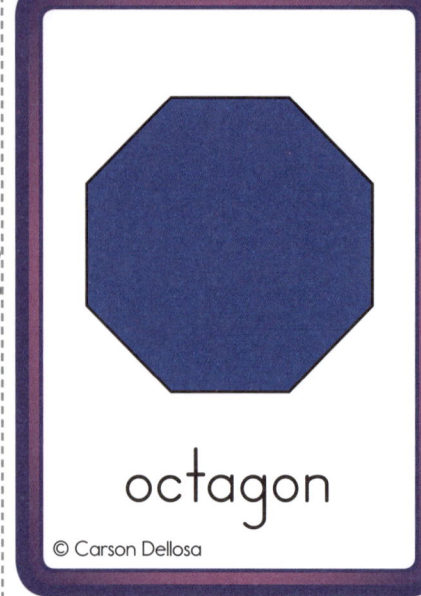
octagon

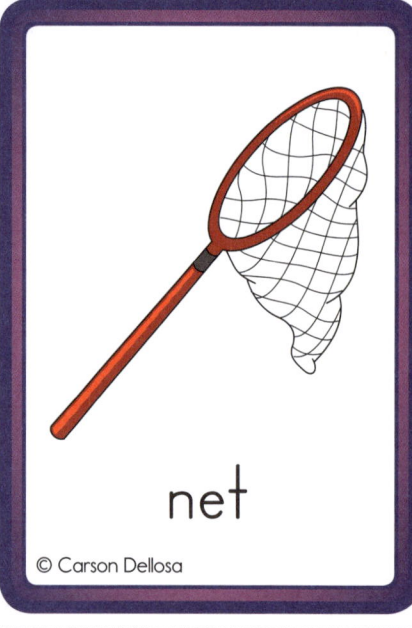
net

mouse

rabbit

quarter

penguin

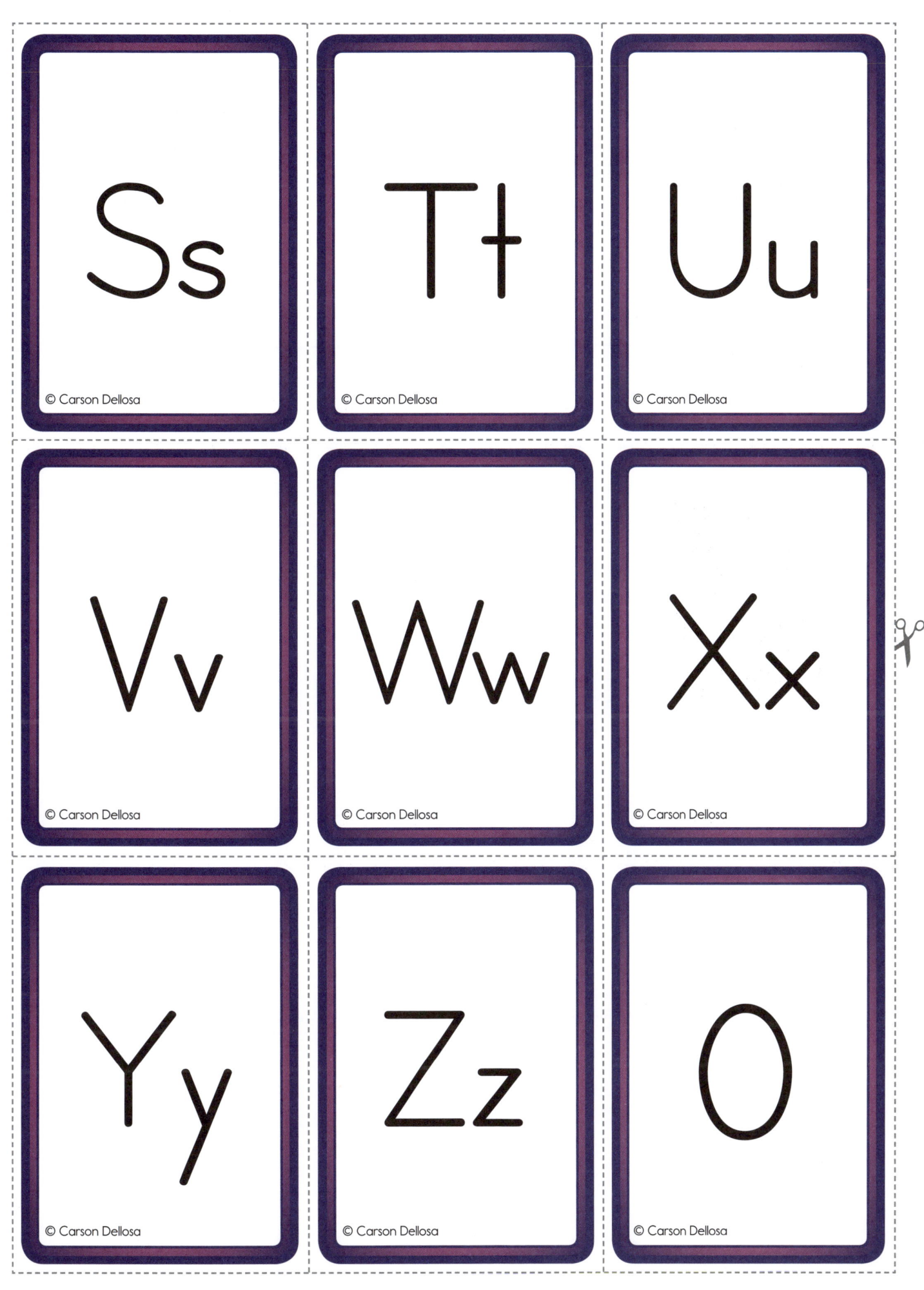

up

tent

socks

X-ray

watch

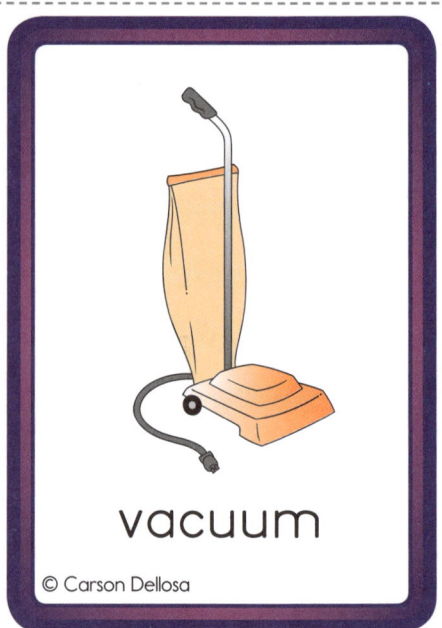

vacuum

zebra

yarn

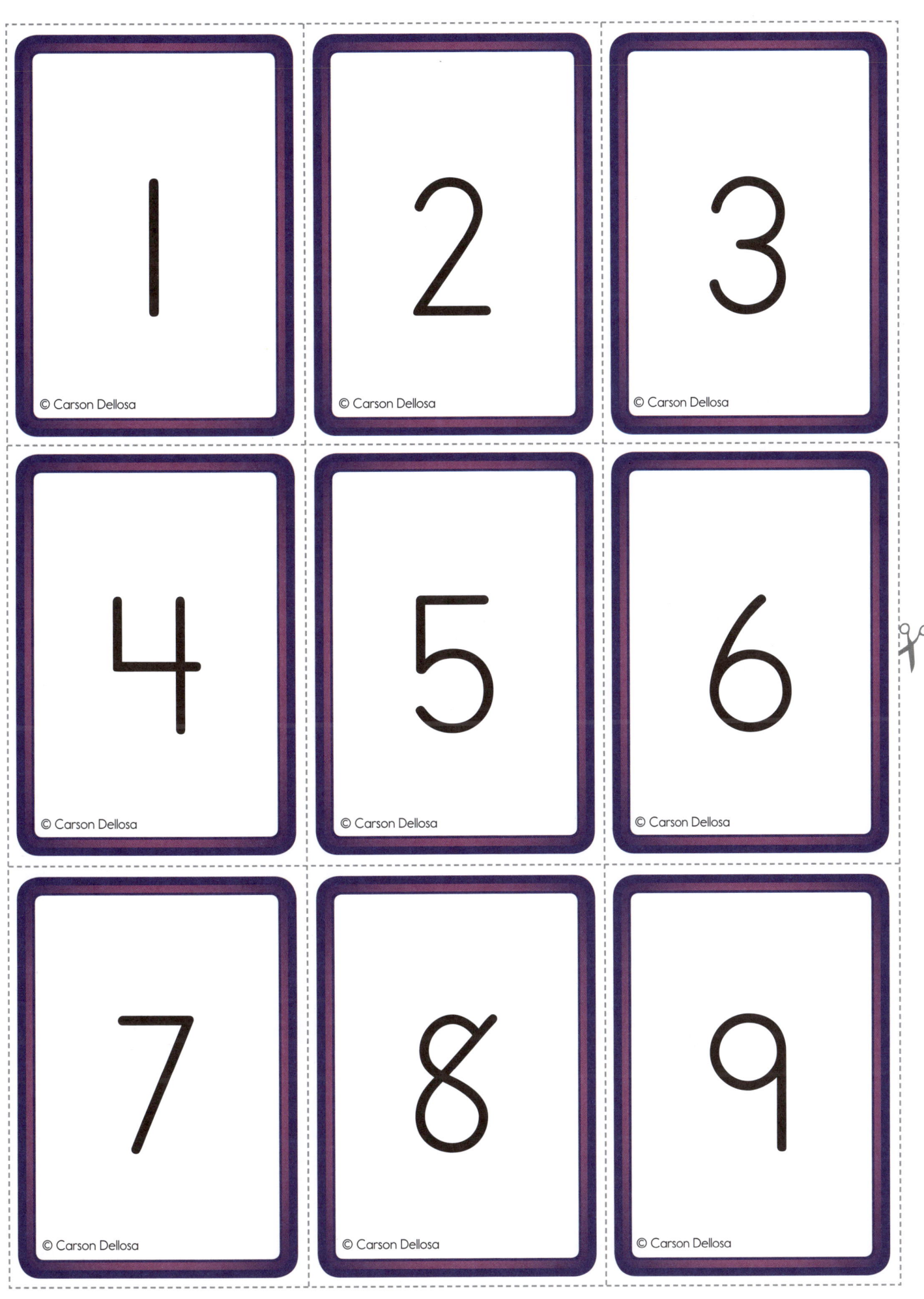

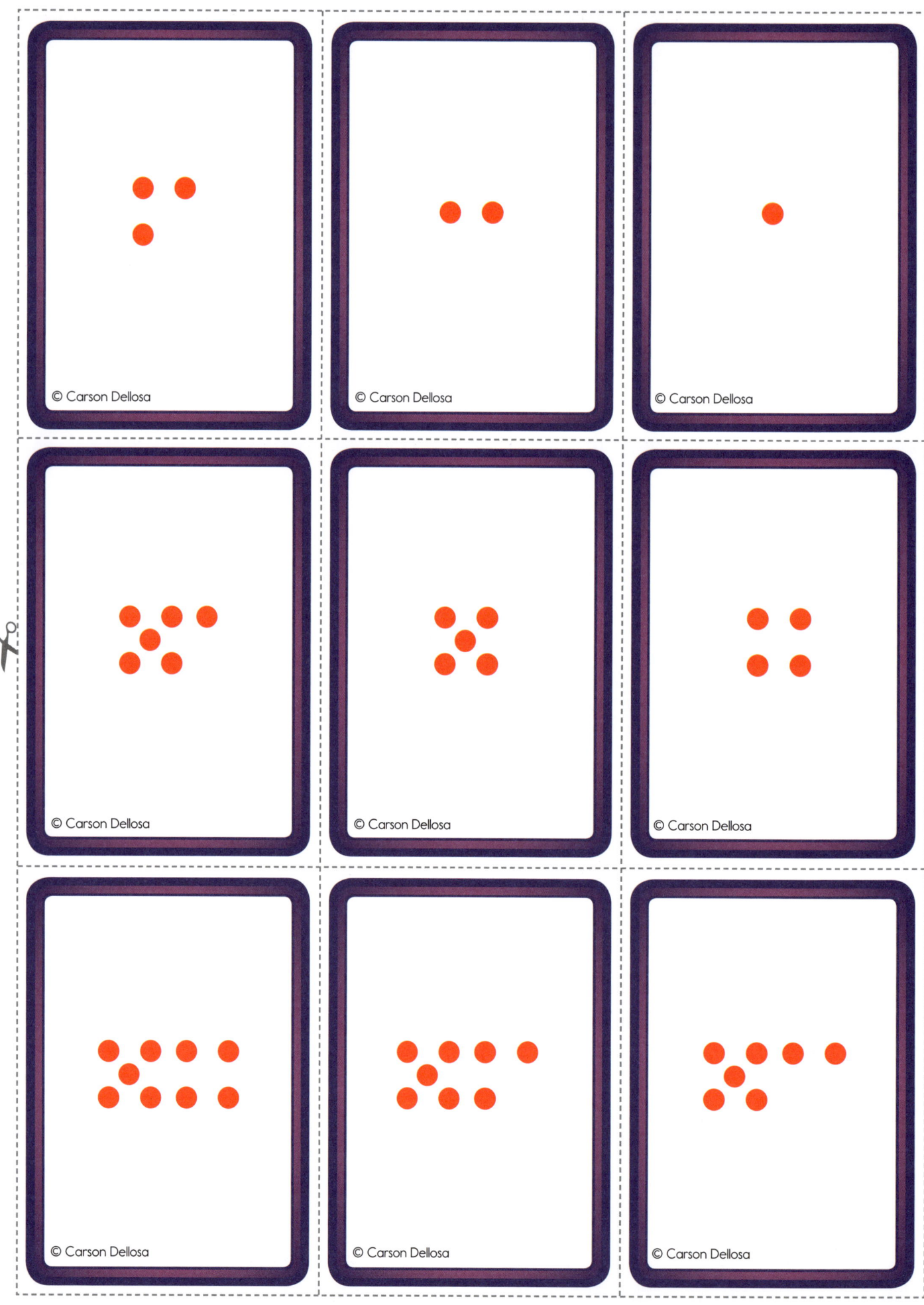

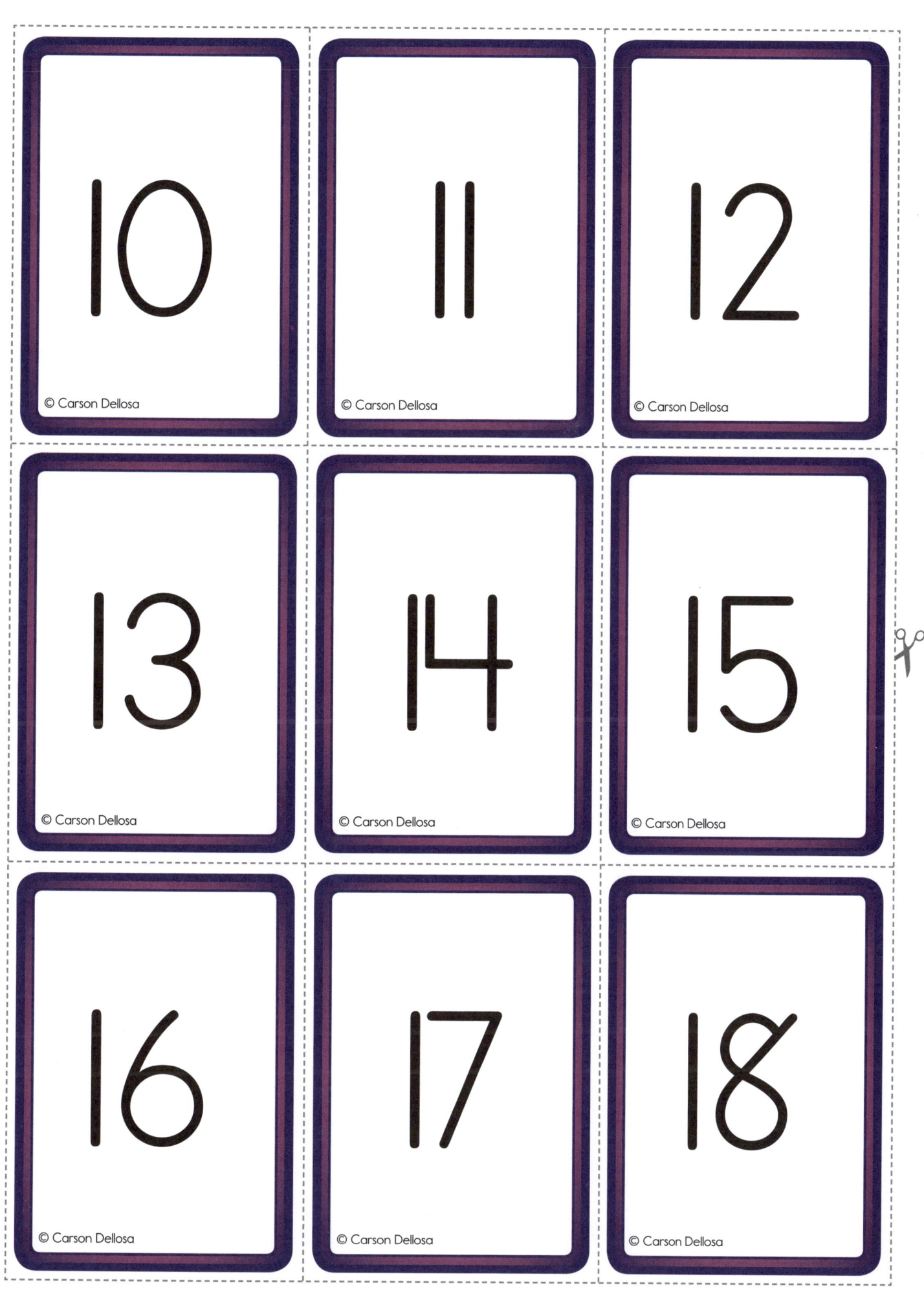

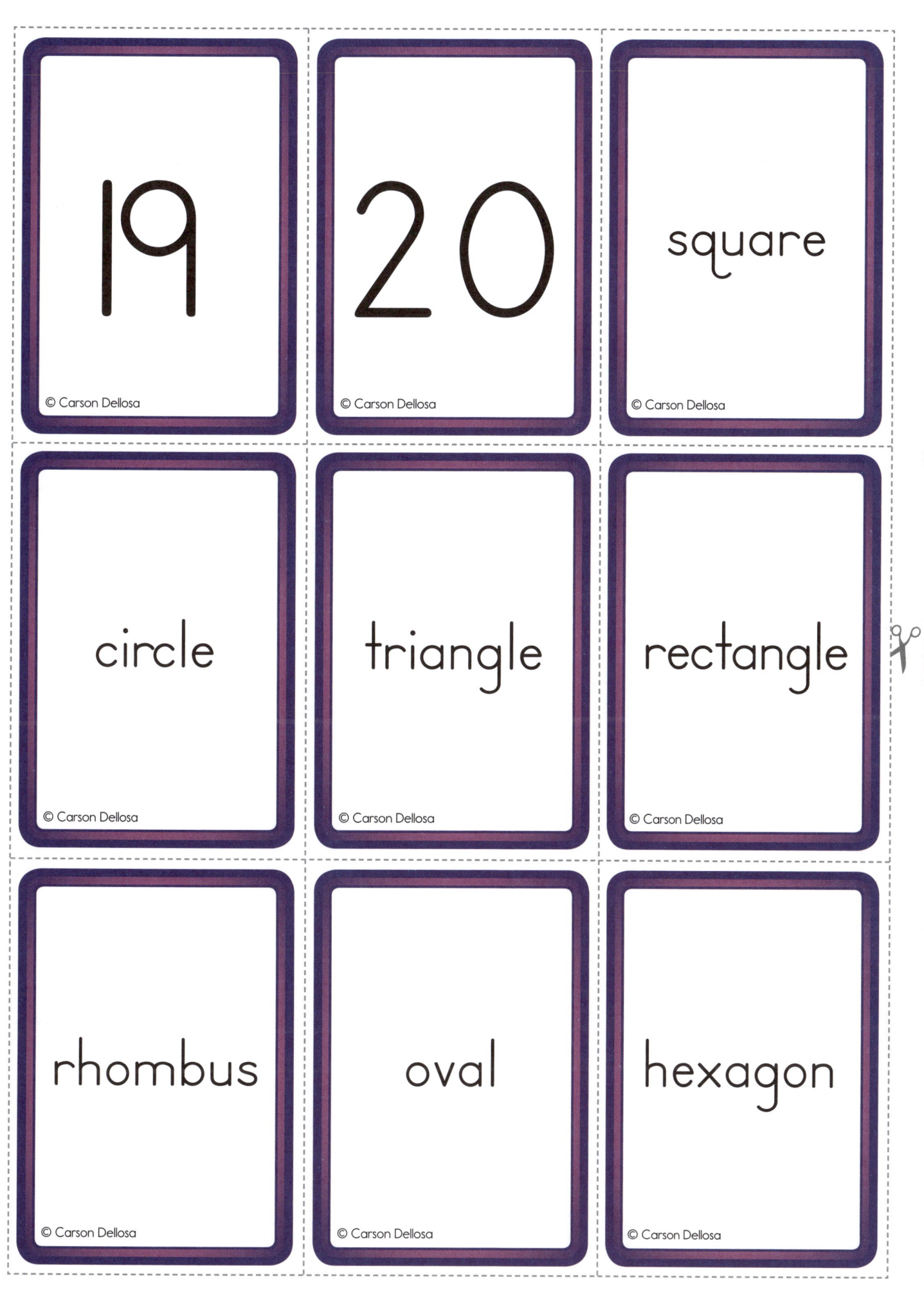

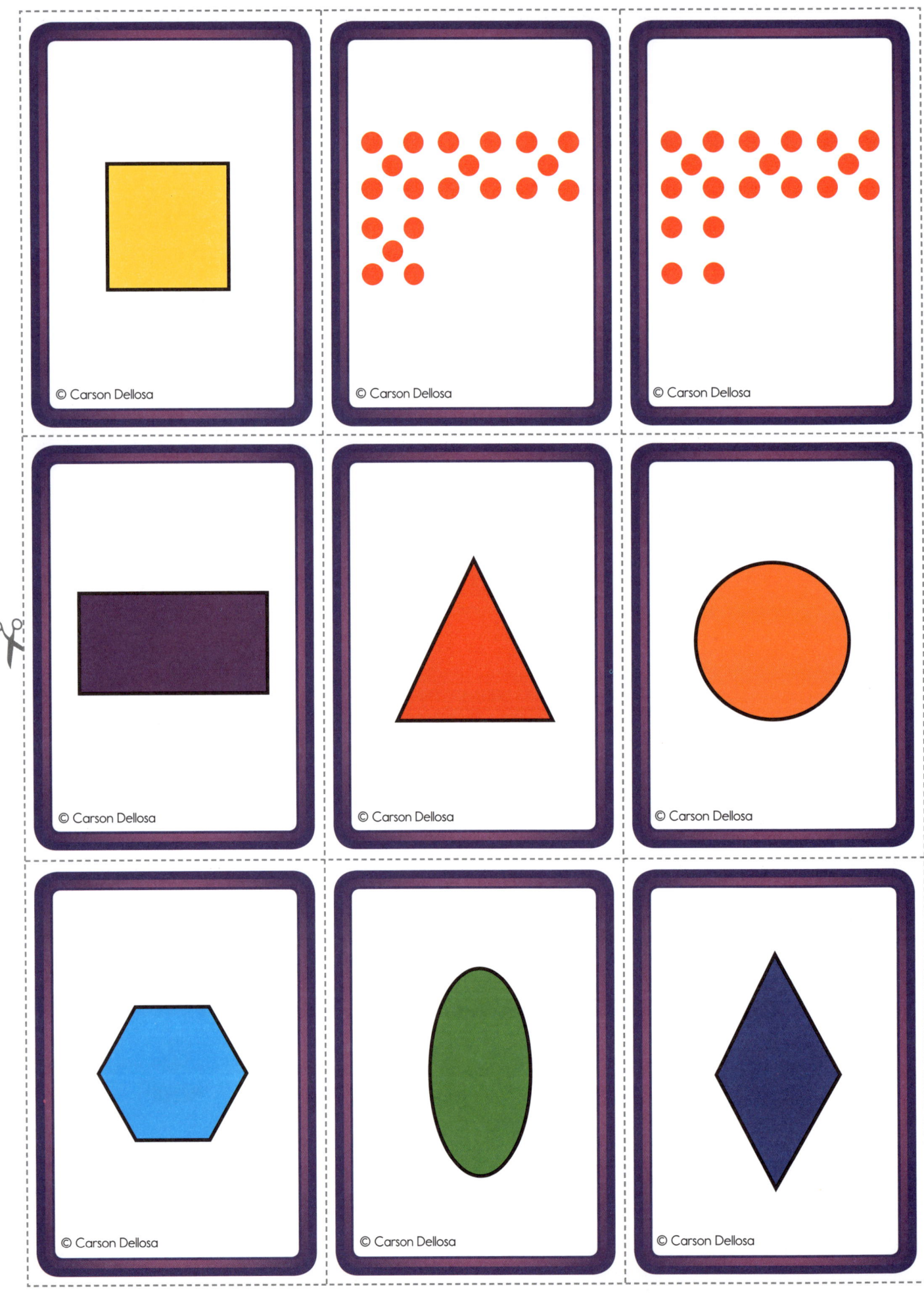

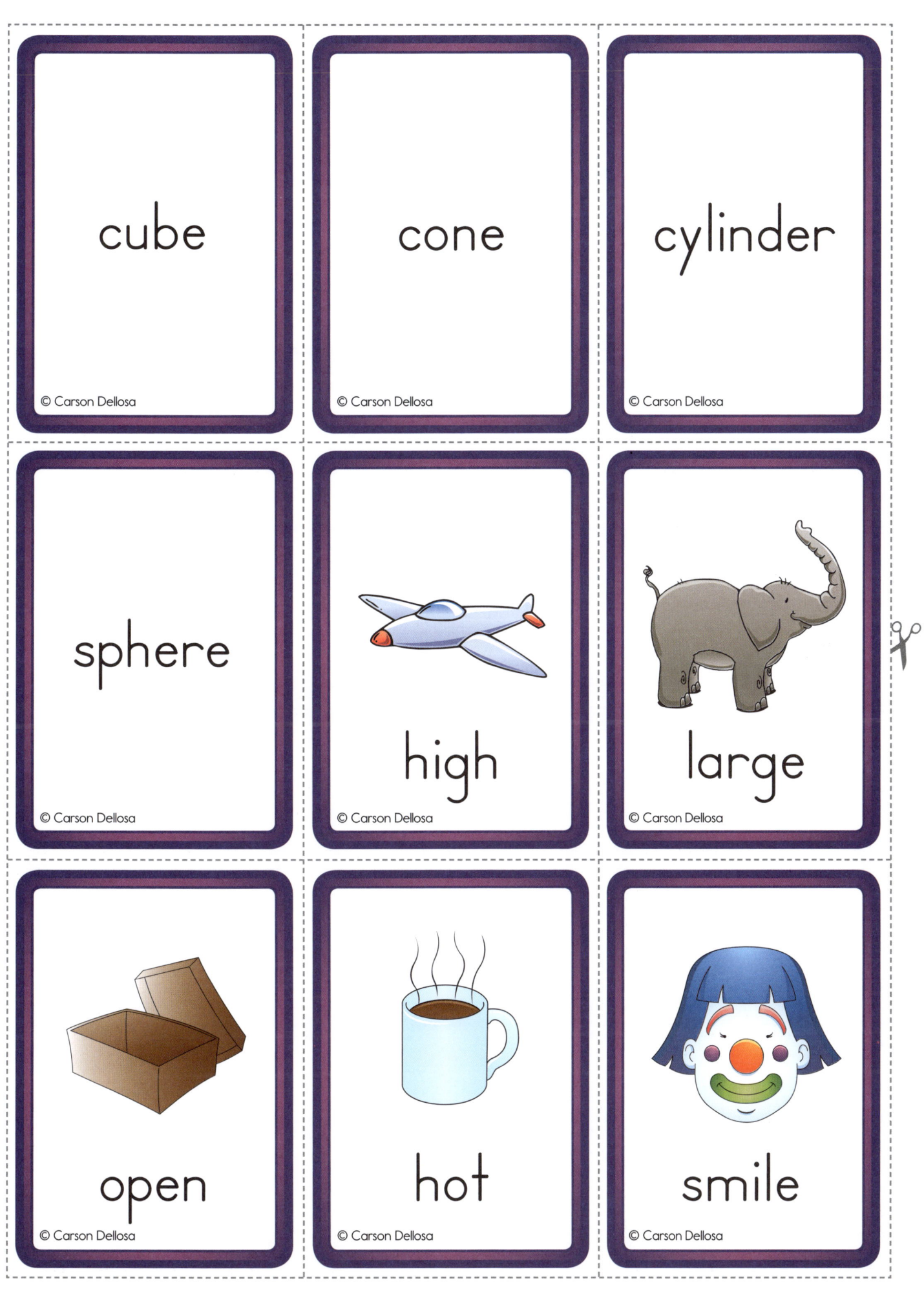

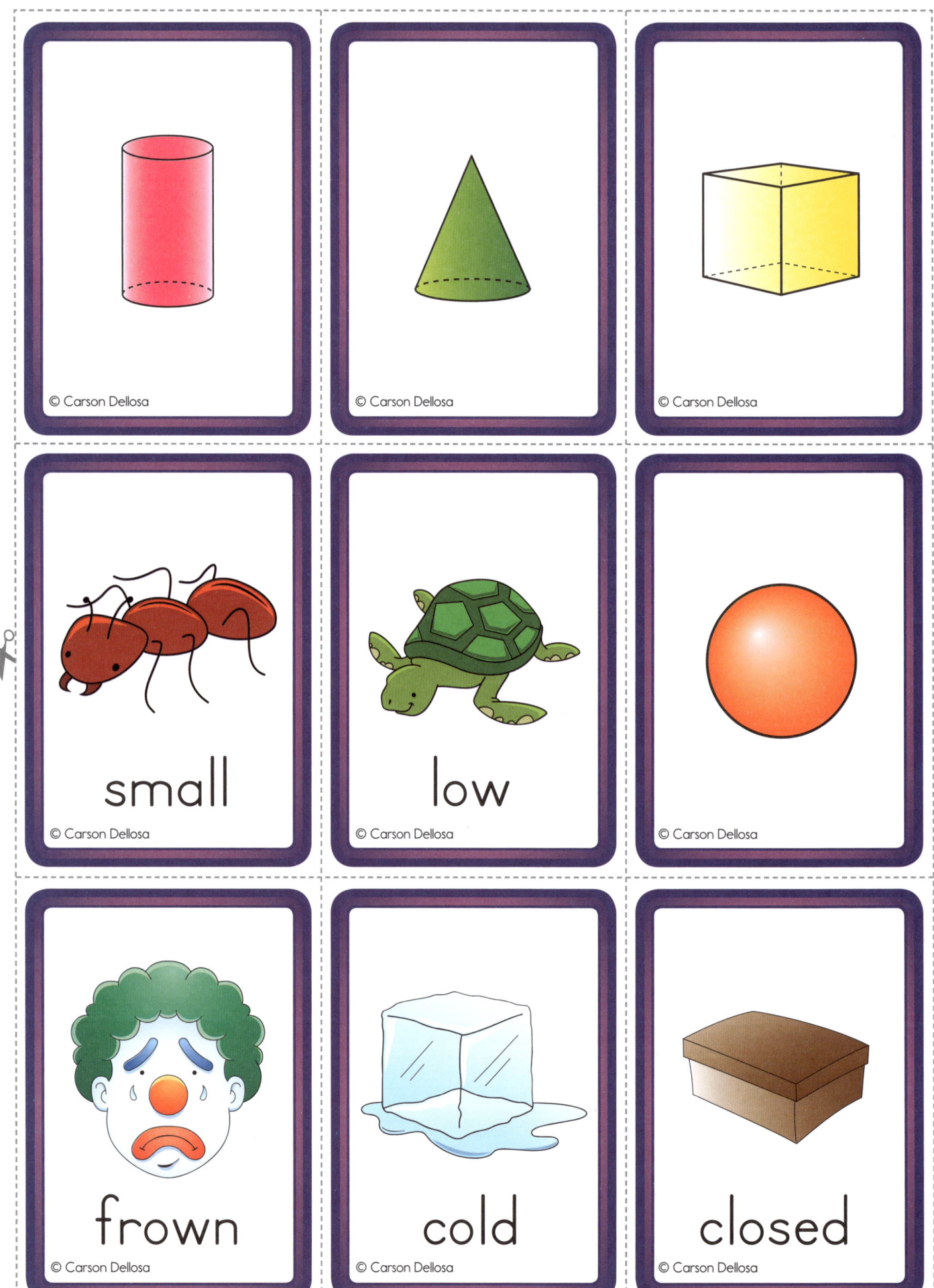

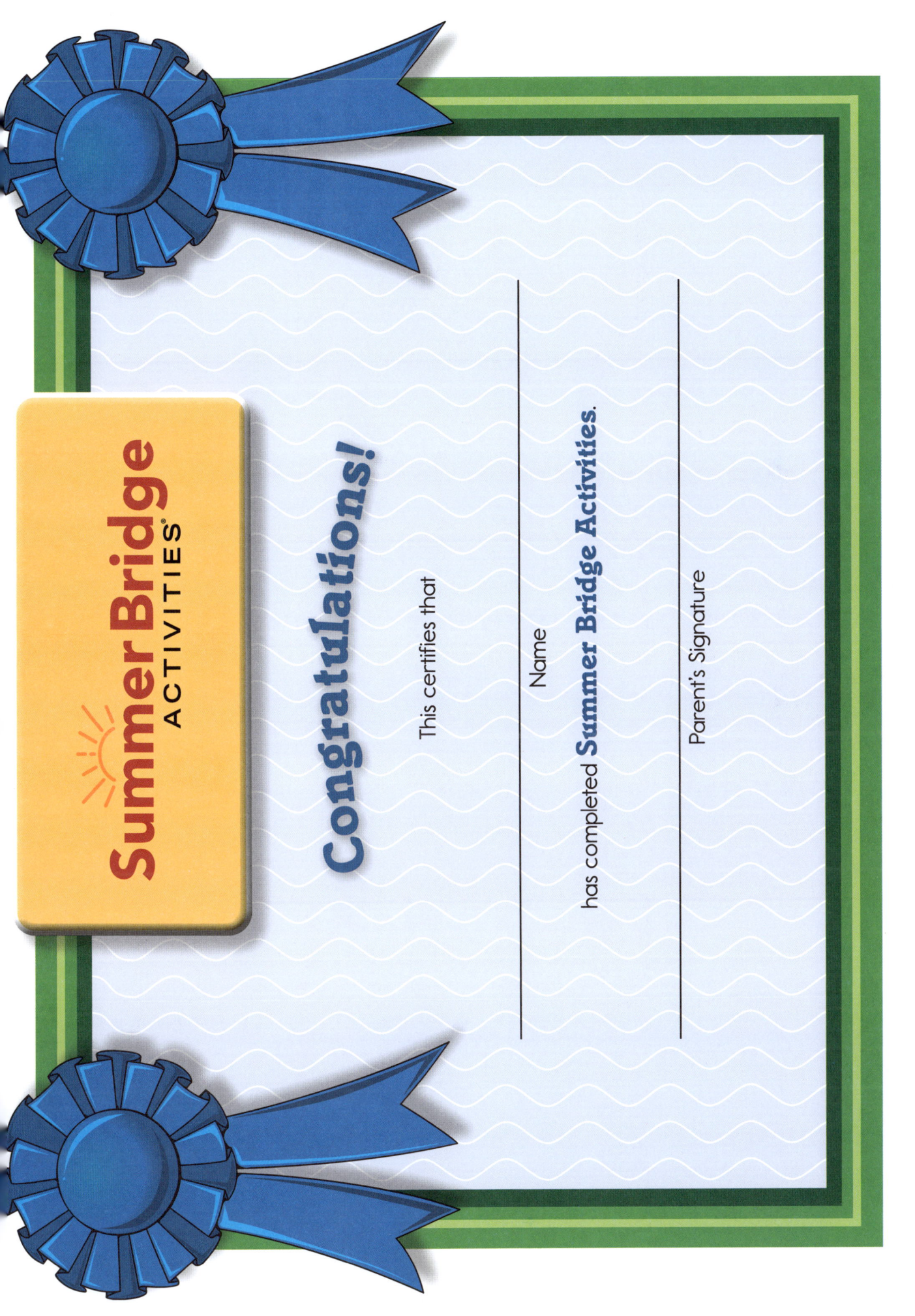